"This life does have its appeal."

"Much better than in the city with its crowds and honking horns, ain't so?" Abe asked.

"That has its appeal, too," Jenna replied.

His heart faltered, surprising him. Why was it acting so oddly? Jenna had made it clear from the day she returned that she'd leave once she'd completed the task Dinah had given her. He shouldn't forget she was a city woman, despite the fact he'd known her as a country kid running around in bare feet.

Abe knew pushing the subject would be useless. "One thing I've been thinking about. Why didn't Dinah create a living trust?"

"If she had, we wouldn't be having fun with her letters." Jenna chuckled.

Abe heard her sarcasm, but he ignored it. "*Fun* may not be the exact term I'd choose, but Dinah is keeping herself in your life, ain't so?"

She looked away, but he was certain he'd seen the sudden glitter of tears in her eyes. He wanted to put his arms around her and offer what scanty comfort he could as she mourned for her *grossmammi*.

He was beginning to realize how vast their shared loss was.

Jo Ann Brown loves stories with happily-ever-after endings. A former military officer, she is thrilled to write about finding that forever love all over again with her characters. She and her husband (her real hero who knows how to fix computer problems quickly when she's on deadline) divide their time between Western Massachusetts and Amish country in Pennsylvania. She loves hearing from readers, so drop her a note at joannbrownbooks.com.

Books by Jo Ann Brown

Love Inspired

An Unlikely Amish Inheritance

Amish of Prince Edward Island

Building Her Amish Dream
Snowbound Amish Christmas
Caring for Her Amish Neighbor
Unexpected Amish Protectors

Green Mountain Blessings

An Amish Christmas Promise
An Amish Easter Wish
An Amish Mother's Secret Past
An Amish Holiday Family

Amish Spinster Club

The Amish Suitor
The Amish Christmas Cowboy
The Amish Bachelor's Baby
The Amish Widower's Twins

Visit the Author Profile page at LoveInspired.com for more titles.

An Unlikely Amish Inheritance

JO ANN BROWN

LOVE INSPIRED
INSPIRATIONAL ROMANCE

LOVE INSPIRED®
INSPIRATIONAL ROMANCE

Recycling programs
for this product may
not exist in your area.

ISBN-13: 978-1-335-93670-7

An Unlikely Amish Inheritance

Copyright © 2024 by Jo Ann Ferguson

Love Inspired
22 Adelaide St. West, 41st Floor
Toronto, Ontario M5H 4E3, Canada
www.LoveInspired.com

Printed in Lithuania

MIX
Paper | Supporting
responsible forestry
FSC® C021394

But this I say, He which soweth sparingly
shall reap also sparingly; and he which
soweth bountifully shall reap also bountifully.
Every man according as he purposeth in his heart,
so let him give; not grudgingly, or of necessity:
for God loveth a cheerful giver.
—*2 Corinthians* 9:6–7

For Barry and Sue
Great neighbors who were here to help us
before the moving van pulled out!

Chapter One

"Abe, *komm* see! There's a robot in the yard!"

At his youngest sister's excited voice, Abe Bontranger looked up from where he'd been hooking the portable milking machine to the last of the twenty cows he was tending in the barn. He glanced out the door, but couldn't see anything other than the barn's long shadow across the Maryland morning's dewy grass. He frowned when Zoe, with her twin brother, Zeke, zipped past the cows who turned their heads to see what the commotion was. The five-year-olds, his youngest siblings, didn't recognize the concept of moderation.

Which was a *gut* thing, he told himself. Kids should run around and have fun. They shouldn't worry about the future.

Unlike his childhood. As the oldest of eleven children, he'd been responsible for his siblings since he was the twins' age. His parents worked long hours at Barnwood Mills, building their business at the same time they'd built their family. His only escape—then and now—had been visiting Dinah Shetler's farm. The woman, who was old enough to be his *grossmammi*, had taught him about animals and crops and how to run a farm after he'd told her he wanted to be a farmer instead of building sheds and playsets as his *daed* did.

"Abe! Abe! Abe!" called both twins. Their bare feet slapped the barn floor.

Putting out his arms to cut off the wild run of the dark-haired *kinder*, he caught one against each side. They wiggled, but he didn't let them escape.

"You know better than to run and shout in the barn when the cows are being milked," he chided.

"There's a robot in the yard!" Zoe's eyes held excitement.

"With a dog. Big as a horse," added her twin. His name was Ezekiel, like their *daed*'s, but nobody had ever called him anything other than Zeke.

"Remember what I said." Abe used a stern tone. "Remember what I said about exaggerating."

The twins exchanged a disgusted glance, then Zoe said, "No eggs-arating, Abe. There's a robot. I saw her with my own eyes!"

"And a big, big dog," Zeke insisted.

Abe tried not to shudder. He didn't trust dogs, especially large ones.

"Really big," Zeke went on when Abe didn't answer. "Big as a horse." When Abe frowned at him, his voice dropped. "Maybe as big as a miniature horse. With three legs."

Sliding the milker away from the cow, so he could get right to work after he calmed the twins, he took them by the hand. He was surprised when their steps faltered as they neared the open door. What had they seen? Not a robot and giant three-legged dog, but they'd seen *something*.

"It's okay." He gave their hands a squeeze.

"Stay with us." Zoe didn't make it a question.

"*Ja.*" He raised his chin so they didn't see his grimace while he led them through the door. Why didn't his parents realize how much they were missing while focused on their business?

"There!" Zoe pointed toward where a white pickup was parked.

Whose was it?

Abe stopped in midstep and stared at an *Englisch* woman coming around the truck. With her was a German shepherd missing its right rear leg. The dog was otherwise a handsome animal with a black snout and patches of the same color in its chestnut coat. It leaned against the blonde woman. Did it have trouble standing on its own or was it trying to comfort the woman, whose face was hidden in her hands as she bent forward? Her shoulders were shaking, bouncing the curls that hung over her shoulders. Was she crying?

So many, including him, had cried when Dinah died last month. Doing Dinah's chores for the past four years had been his way of thanking her for helping him learn to be a farmer. At her funeral in the big white farmhouse, he'd told her he'd make sure her land and animals were taken care of. Once her will was probated, her heirs, who lived on the neighboring farm, had promised he could buy Dinah's property.

"Abe," whispered Zeke. "Who's that?"

He shook away his grief and looked at the woman again. His gaze riveted on her lush blond curls. He'd never seen hair like that...except on Jenna Rose Shetler.

Could the woman be a grown-up Jenna Rose Shetler, Dinah's *kins-kind*? She wasn't the gangly *Englisch* girl he remembered from her annual visits with her plain *grossmammi*. She was a beautiful woman dressed in a soft brown leather jacket and denims. One thing hadn't changed. Her blond hair, a natural shade the color of young corn, was wildly untamed.

When they'd been *kinder*, she'd reminded him of a sparkler, burning hot and glittering for a brief moment and then gone until next summer. Abe knew he couldn't blame her, but he hadn't wanted to have to watch over another kid. He'd told himself at summer's end how glad he was when she left her *grossmammi*'s farm in Sweetwater, Maryland, to go off to some faraway place. Atlanta. Chicago. Seattle. Boston. Other places. He'd lost track, and he wouldn't have admitted how envious he'd been of her carefree life.

"Who's that, Abe?" asked his five-year-old brother again.

From somewhere, he pulled out a smile and plastered it on his face. "I'm going to find out."

"Do you see the dog?" his sister asked.

"I do."

"Can I pet her?"

"It's a boy dog." His smile became more genuine, but he grew somber again. "Let's see if it's okay. Some dogs like to bite. Remember?"

The kids looked at his right hand and nodded. He clenched his fingers, though he was too familiar with how inflexible his ring finger and pinkie had become after a dog had attacked him.

"Go and play on the tire swing while I check." Abe released the twins' hands and strode toward where the woman stood next to the mailbox. His youngest siblings raced to the old tire swing in the side yard. "Can I help you?"

"Abe?" the woman asked as she tightened her hold on the dog's leash.

It wasn't a massive dog, but he could see muscles beneath its fur. He expected the German shepherd to growl but it remained silent. That stillness was almost more threatening, and he stopped, not wanting to come within range of the dog's teeth.

"Jenna Rose?" He asked the question burning his lips since he'd seen her corkscrew curls. "What are you doing here after all these years?"

Grossmammi Dinah had warned her to be careful what she prayed for because she might just get it.

Jenna Shetler should have listened, but she'd ignored that warning as she had other advice her Amish grandmother had offered. Every summer, Jenna had explored the house, delighting in a staircase that went nowhere and doors that no longer opened. She checked out the fields and the Pocomoke River that ran along the rear of the property and south toward Chesapeake Bay. She'd spent every summer with her grandmother until she was fifteen. She'd visited occasionally in the ensuing fifteen years. Living three hours away in Philadelphia, she could have made the trip south—as she had yesterday—to visit. She hadn't, spending her time focused on achieving her goals as a police officer. Now her grandmother was dead, and her career hung by a very slender thread.

She'd tried praying for a new purpose in her life, and an answer had come, though she wasn't sure God had heard her prayers. Because the response had come through her late grandmother's attorney. He'd explained that *Grossmammi* Dinah had asked for her to serve as the estate's executor. So she was at the farm outside the sleepy town of Sweetwater on Maryland's Eastern Shore.

She hadn't guessed the first person she'd meet would be Abe Bontranger. Born and raised Amish, he wore a straw hat as well as black suspenders over his light green shirt. The same type of plain clothing he'd worn when he'd been her partner in crime during their youth. She'd almost caught up with him in height when they were eleven, but by the time she returned the next summer, he was more than five inches taller. He'd kept growing—his head must top out at least three inches over six feet. He needed a haircut because several wayward locks dropped over his wire-rimmed glasses and into his gray eyes.

"Jenna Rose?" Abe asked again, yanking her thoughts out of the past. She was grateful because it was far too easy to get sucked into the moment she'd let her guard down and almost killed herself and her canine partner.

"I go by Jenna now." She glanced at the dog by her side and tilted her head so her right ear was toward Abe. Since she'd been too close to the detonation, the hearing in her left ear had been weak, almost as if she were listening through a tissue curtain. "This is Buddy. My partner."

"Partner?"

"We worked together in Philadelphia. K-9."

Abe's eyes widened behind his glasses. "Dinah mentioned you're a cop."

"You look surprised. Why? I wasn't raised plain."

"I know, but your *grossmammi* was Old Order Amish, and none of us would ever use a gun except when hunting to put food on the table."

"I'm a cop, and so was Buddy."

She smiled at the stunning German shepherd. He gave her his goofy doggy grin, and she patted his head. It amazed her as much now as the first time she'd met him how the dog who acted like a spoiled pet while off duty was all business when they searched for a bomb. For Buddy, catching the scent of explosive materials was a prelude to playtime. When he'd found the source, whether in training or on the job, his reward had been fifteen minutes of playing with his favorite chewy toy, a hard rubber squirrel.

When he nuzzled her arm with his cool nose, she knew he wanted training time so he could gnaw on the squirrel. In the past three months, now that she was steady on her feet, she'd been helping him learn to track the odors left on clothing or shoes or on the ground. He approached the task with the enthusiasm he'd once had for bomb-sniffing. Had he forgotten how a bomb had gone off in a shopping mall and they'd been caught in the blast because she'd been distracted by a dress in a window that looked like one she'd seen her estranged half sister wear a few years ago? She'd pondered—for a minute or two—if there was any way she could bridge the chasm between her and Susan. The minute or two had been too long. The bomb had exploded, leaving her and her K-9 partner injured.

A low whine came from Buddy, and Jenna forced another smile. The dog was aware of every iota of her body language. Buddy didn't like it when she was downhearted. The whine was his way of pleading with her to pay attention to him.

In order to escape her thoughts, Jenna opened the mailbox by the drive. Pulling out a stack of mail, she held it close to her heart. How she wished she could run inside as she used to do and present the mail to *Grossmammi* Dinah as if it were the most exciting gift in the world!

Reaching into the bag she'd left on the truck's rear bumper, she found the keys she'd been given by her grandmother's attorney. Keys for a house she couldn't remember ever being locked.

"Nobody locks their houses in Sweetwater," *Grossmammi* Dinah had remarked. "It's not like in the cities where you've lived. There, you don't know your neighbors. Not like we do here."

Jenna couldn't argue with that since her mother's radio career had kept the family on the move, sometimes more than once in a year. Listeners around the country knew her mother, Evelyn, as Marla in the Morning, advice guru and upbeat best friend to share your morning coffee with while hearing the latest music and news updates. Her parents, as well as her sister and her sister's family, lived in Las Vegas now, but they'd resided in many cities, big and small.

The one constant in her life had been this white house and *Grossmammi* Dinah. Now that had changed because her grandmother was gone.

Tears blurred the sight of well-used rocking chairs on the broad screened-in porch. Jenna had to handle the hideous task of parceling out her grandmother's possessions. When she was done...

Throughout her life, she'd known what she wanted to do next.

Now she had no idea.

Abe had so many questions, but as he watched how fragile Jenna appeared as she held the pile of mail close, he reminded himself she'd just lost one of the most important people in her life.

"I didn't expect to see you here now." He wished he could retract the trite words as soon as he spoke them.

"I'm here to—" She glanced over her shoulder as a bright red pickup pulled into the drive and parked behind her truck. Her eyes narrowed as doors opened, and the Rickaboughs stepped out.

Daryl and Geneva, who were a generation older than Abe, were a foot shorter. Like Jenna's *daed*, their parents had jumped the fence. The couple, who were related to Jenna somehow, were almost identical in height, breadth and coloring. Geneva had streaks of gray through her medium brown hair while Daryl's was thinning.

Abe found Geneva caustic. Daryl was okay, though he followed his wife's edicts. By helping Dinah with her chores, Abe had saved the Rickaboughs from having to take care of two properties. They owned a chicken farm about a half mile away. His agreement, in the wake of Dinah's death, was that he'd continue to do the milking and other work until the will was settled. The Rickaboughs had assured him they would put the pay he should have gotten toward a down payment on the farm.

He looked from the couple to Jenna. She hadn't told him what had brought her to Sweetwater. Was she here to get what she thought she'd inherited from Dinah? If so, she was wasting her time. Daryl and his wife were inheriting everything. Everyone in Sweetwater knew that.

Jenna isn't from Sweetwater.

He almost gave his own thought a "duh." Sweetwater had been nothing but a whistle-stop in her life.

As Abe opened his mouth, Daryl butted in with, "Is that you, Jenna Rose?"

"It is, and you are—?"

Abe was astonished for a moment, then remembered that Daryl hadn't been in Sweetwater when Jenna had visited. As a teen, he'd lived in Delaware.

"I'm Daryl, your father's cousin." He grinned, but kept glancing at her dog. Unlike most farmers in the area, the Rickaboughs didn't have a dog, and Abe had heard Geneva didn't like them.

"I've heard of you," she replied, her voice cautious. Abe wondered what exactly she'd heard about Daryl.

"Good to see you, Jenna Rose." Daryl didn't seem put off by her comment. "You should have visited before your grandmother died instead of afterwards. Or were you trying to avoid her matchmaking? The old girl was disappointed you're still single."

If the words hurt her, and Abe was sure they did, Jenna gave no sign. "I'm here to take care of *Grossmammi* Dinah's estate."

Daryl's smile vanished. "Take care of it? How?"

Jenna's poise cracked for a moment, and Abe couldn't forget how she'd been crying by the road. She swallowed hard twice before she replied. "To be honest, I'm not sure. Instructions for what I'm to do are supposed to be here waiting for me." She looked at the mail she carried. "In a letter that is supposed to arrive here this week. The first of six weekly letters with instructions I need to follow as my grandmother's executor."

"Dinah made you the executor?" Geneva asked.

Abe tensed. Was Geneva about to go on one of her verbal rampages? He'd witnessed her lambasting people with acidic words. When Buddy sniffed at her, she stepped away with a disdainful expression.

"I'm as surprised she named me executor as you are." Jenna put her hand on the dog's head.

"So when do we get the farm?" Daryl said, trying not to grin.

Abe held his breath. He had an interest in the will, too. The sooner the Rickaboughs could get the estate out of probate, the sooner Abe could make the farm his own. He'd already put in a lot of long hours of sweat equity, taking care of the animals and fixing the buildings and tending the fields.

"I don't know, Daryl," Jenna said. "*Grossmammi* Dinah's will has some odd provisions."

"Like what?" Geneva's voice was sharp.

Too sharp, he knew, when Buddy shifted between Geneva and Jenna, his movements a bit uneven because of his missing leg. Three-legged dogs weren't that unusual in farming country where there was dangerous farm equipment. What had happened to him in the city?

"Six letters will be sent." Jenna acted as if Geneva had been pleasant. "One a week. Each explains which bequests *Grossmammi* Dinah wants made that week."

"That's absurd!" Daryl spoke an octave above his normal voice. "What kind of prank are you trying to pull, Jenna Rose? We don't have time for games."

She remained calm. Abe wasn't surprised. She was a cop, after all.

"It's no game," Jenna replied. "I couldn't have come up with this bizarre idea. It's *Grossmammi* Dinah's doing."

"Why six different bequests?" Geneva asked.

"I don't know. Ken Geisinger, her attorney, doesn't know, but he says the will is sound even though its provisions are the most unusual he's ever seen."

"Ken?" Abe turned to the Rickaboughs. "You know him. He's honest."

Jenna spoke before her cousins could answer. "He's been as blindsided as we are. He knew about the envelopes, but not what they contain. He advised me to follow the steps as she requested."

"Who gets the farm?" Daryl asked.

"I don't know. I've got to assume the answer will be in one of the letters."

"She promised us the farm!"

"*Grossmammi* Dinah never broke a promise." Tears glittered in her eyes, reminding Abe this wasn't just about the land and buildings.

"This is nonsense," Daryl blustered.

"Absolute nonsense." His wife glared at Jenna so fiercely Abe wouldn't have been astonished to see two holes burned through her.

He shared Daryl and Geneva's frustration. Six weeks. A month and a half. So many Bible verses urged patience and for them to wait on God's time. It seemed like *Grossmammi* Dinah had been inspired to devise a lesson that would require them to do that.

Why?

Something else he couldn't answer. When Daryl began to snarl at Jenna again, Abe interrupted, "Jenna is only the messenger."

Geneva's brows lowered, and Daryl put a hand on her arm. "You're right, Abe. Sorry, Jenna Rose. This is a real shock."

"For me, too," Jenna said. "By the way, I go by Jenna now."

"Got it." Daryl tried to smile and failed. "Can you stay in Sweetwater for six weeks? Aren't you a cop or something like that?"

"I've got the time." She shrugged again. "Once I get the letter and read it over, I'll let you know what it says. Okay?"

"Okay." He eyed his wife. "Right, Geneva?"

Abe's breath sifted out of him when Geneva nodded. Her lips straightened as she turned away and headed toward the red truck.

Daryl hesitated, then followed.

Abe realized he was alone with Jenna and her dog. Beating a hasty retreat to the barn would be his wisest move. "Jen—"

"Abe," Jenna said at the same time.

"Go ahead," he urged as they walked toward the house.

"Why are *you* here on the farm?"

"I'm milking. I've been doing the chores for about four years."

"Oh." Though he could sense her curiosity about why her grandmother had given him the task—or why he'd even asked to do it—she said, "I should get unpacked."

"You're really staying here?"

"The letters are coming to the farm. I need to be here to get them." She turned to the steps and raised her right foot, leaning on the rail.

The ancient board gave a warning creak, which was swallowed by a shriek from Zoe and Zeke as she took another step, lifting her left foot.

"Told you! She's a robot!" squealed Zoe.

He wasn't sure if his little sister was thrilled or terrified. She ran toward them and clutched on to him, but her gaze was riveted on the metal rod where Jenna's left leg should have been.

What had happened to Jenna's leg?

He realized he'd said that aloud when Jenna looked at her left shoe. "It's my prosthesis."

"So you're a robot?" asked Zoe.

"Afraid not."

Disappointment filled Zoe's voice. "It'd be so cool if you were a robot."

Zeke piped up. "You've got a *metal* leg?"

"Yes."

Abe waited for her to add more. When she didn't, he knew he'd be smart to keep his mouth closed, too. He couldn't. "What happened?"

"A bomb blew up." She put her hand on Buddy's head. "Don't worry. Nothing else has changed."

As he watched her climb the steps with more ease than

he'd guessed she could, he knew she was wrong. Jenna Shetler, who had come to Sweetwater each summer when they were kids, was back.

That changed everything.

Chapter Two

After crossing the wide screened porch with Buddy, Jenna stepped through the front door and into her childhood. Her ears strained to hear *Grossmammi* Dinah's welcome echoing along the tall ceiling of the entrance hall. Her grandmother hadn't had what anyone would call a melodious voice. Not by a long shot. Dinah Shetler had gotten into trouble as a plain teen when she'd won a hogcalling contest. Plain people didn't believe in taking part in *Englisch* competitions, but Grossmammi Dinah hadn't been able to resist joining the fun. Jenna had never doubted the story was true. The bellow of "Jen-n-n-n-n-a" had reached across the fields, even through the racket of a bunch of kids shouting at the top of their lungs.

Now there was silence. Just as there had been at the cemetery where *Grossmammi* Dinah had been buried with a stone that was identical to all the others. Jenna had stopped there on her way to the farm, but couldn't come up with a single thing to say. So many words ricocheted through her heart. None of them reached her lips.

Now she stood in the silent house. Its heartbeat was gone as if it had, after more than two hundred years, died along with her grandmother.

Being maudlin wouldn't help. When Jenna took a deep breath, her nose wrinkled. The house smelled of June heat and a dustiness that reminded her of an old book. She wondered when someone had last been inside. Probably for the funeral last month. The funeral she'd missed. If she'd attended after coming so close to dying herself last year, she would have had horrific nightmares. Or worse, seeing her grandmother closed into a wooden box and put in the ground, her life snatched away as Jenna's nearly had been, would have triggered what she called "time-outs." She'd suffered them since she'd awakened in the hospital, her leg so mangled it had to be removed a few days later.

Every time-out was the same. First the world contracted until she was within a sphere of misty shadows. Scenes played out in the fog, scenes that were a mixture of truth and fantasy because she saw things she couldn't have seen. The bomb exploded in slo-mo, the cloud of shrapnel and ball bearings and smoke billowing out and consuming her and Buddy. Next came her grabbing her partner and tugging him beside her on the mall's cold, hard floor, hoping her bulletproof vest would save them. It was followed by what appeared to be an EMT leaning over her and the German shepherd who lay there like extras in a slasher film.

Then seconds later, she would be hit by a tsunami of guilt. Guilt that she'd been thinking of mending fences with her estranged sister instead of her job. Guilt that she'd failed Buddy. Guilt that, at the moment of the explosion, she hadn't thought of anyone but herself and her dog. Yes, she shouted a warning that there was a bomb that was about to explode, but hadn't checked if the other cops had gotten to safety. Instead she'd wrapped her body around Buddy, unsure if they'd survive.

At the hospital, when she'd been visited by her fellow officers, she hadn't been able to meet their eyes. When she returned to work, it got worse. It…

Jenna squeezed her eyes closed. *Think of now*, she ordered herself as her therapist had taught. *Now.*

Buddy padded past her, sticking his nose under the oak

hall tree and then around the base of the curving stairs. He shot her a look for permission. When she waved him away, he headed into the living room on the left, his tail wagging like a flag in a high wind.

In addition to the hall tree with its oval mirror and small seat, there was a long pew set against the stairwell. The walls were a flyspecked tan with decals stuck on them. They were verses about family, friends and having a faith. Her grandmother had put them in every room. She wondered if she should have the walls repainted before the house was put on the market, then remembered it might not be her decision.

Jenna walked into the kitchen. It was a tribute to pre–World War II design with a few anachronisms, including a mixer and a coffee maker, and sayings on the walls. She remembered her last visit when her grandmother had shown her the two solar panels she'd installed, as soon as the district's *Ordnung* was changed to allow them, so she could have a few electrical appliances in her kitchen, though the overhead light was propane. The porcelain sink and its attached drainboard were almost five feet wide and set into a metal cabinet that had been painted dark brown. It contrasted with the curved-top white refrigerator and the stove with its four burners on one side and a counter space of its own above the large oven.

A small rectangular table with a blue laminate top and shiny metal legs was surrounded by four matching chairs. The plastic seats were worn, but not ripped. The furniture and some appliances had been in the house when *Grossmammi* Dinah had moved in a year after her wedding. She'd kept each pristine.

Jenna put the mail on the table. Going to the sink to get a drink of water, she turned on the tap. Nothing came out. She opened the refrigerator door. Inside it was empty…and warm.

Ken hadn't mentioned the propane that ran the refrigerator and stove had been turned off. If someone had done that, why hadn't they stopped the mail?

Grumbling, she went to the cellar door. The switch for the propane tank was in the cellar. She opened the door and paused. The wooden steps were uneven, and one about halfway down was missing. Worse, there was no banister. She was aware of how alone she was in the house. If she fell on the stairs, how long would it take for someone to notice?

Her steps, as she returned to the entry hall, were stiff as they often were when she'd been driving a distance. She found it galling to have to see if anyone else was still around. She was used to doing things on her own. When bugs needed killing or a dare was thrown out, she'd been the one to do it. That had stood her in good stead when she'd gone through the police academy and worked a tough section of the city. She'd depended on herself when she'd applied for the K-9 program. Releasing a little of that self-reliance had been vital once she and Buddy began training together to locate bombs.

Now she'd been thwarted by a simple set of stairs.

The door opened before she could reach it. Abe came in. When Buddy poked his head out to see who'd arrived, Abe froze, his hands gripping the handles of her suitcases that had been in the truck.

"It's okay, Buddy," Jenna said. "Just Abe."

As the dog disappeared into the living room, Abe's mouth tightened, showing he didn't like being referred to as "just Abe." She could have explained she and Buddy used a simple list of commands that communicated a lot of information fast. Saying someone's name after "just" was the way Buddy understood the person was no danger to her or to him.

She didn't elaborate. Answering questions about the German shepherd was the quickest way to bring more questions about why she had a prosthesis above her left knee. She wasn't ashamed. She just didn't want to have to satisfy everybody's curiosity.

Or admit the injuries—both hers and Buddy's—were her fault.

"I figured you'd want these." Abe held the luggage as easily as if the large suitcases were filled with air. "Are you staying in your regular room?"

She almost asked him how he knew which room she'd stayed in; then she remembered the nights when she'd shinnied down a tree from her window to meet him and other local kids for after-dark games of hide-and-seek.

"I don't know," Jenna replied. "I haven't been upstairs to check what state the rooms are in." When his gaze narrowed in on her left leg, she hurried on, "Are the kids coming in?"

For the first time since he'd entered the house, his face relaxed, and he set her bags on the floor. "It's a treat for them to play on the swing."

"I liked playing on it, too. I liked everything about being here."

He met her eyes. "I should have said this first thing, Jenna. I'm sorry about Dinah. I know how important she was to you."

"She was. If I hadn't come here summers…" She let her voice trail off, not wanting to reveal how visiting her grandmother had given her a break from her family. Her ambitious mother who never was content. Her stepfather who was so laidback he never responded with anything but "Yes, dear" to his wife's announcement they were moving again. Her half sister who was the epitome of the perfect daughter: top of her class, a volunteer for the right organizations, homecoming queen in high school and college. Susan had married the right man, the CEO of a software company whose stock seemed to quadruple in value every quarter. She'd given him a son and a daughter, and they lived in the lovely house they shared with a matched set of French bulldogs. Susan had never put a foot wrong.

Jenna, on the other hand, tripped over her feet often, put her foot in her mouth even more often and had stepped on a lot of toes. Sometimes not regretting it, but toting around enough guilt to drown a blue whale.

"How's your family?" Abe asked as if she'd spoken every thought aloud.

She started to reply, then coughed. "Sorry. I'm dry as dust."

"Do you want me to get you a glass of water?"

"There's no water. I think the water pump's off as well as the propane."

"Do you want me to switch them on?"

"Yes. Yes, please." She added the latter because it seemed like the right thing to do, though she couldn't recall ever saying "please" or "thanks" to Abe years ago. They'd been friends who didn't need such niceties.

Cutting his eyes toward the dining room where Buddy was sniffing at the built-in hutch, which was surrounded by a collection of wall clocks, Abe walked to the cellar door, opened it and headed down. He'd been as obsessed with dogs as she'd been when they were younger, but now he acted leery around Buddy.

What else had changed in his life since the last time she'd seen him? He had kids with him. Were they his? They looked like him. He hadn't mentioned a wife, and he was clean-shaven. She was sure Amish men grew beards once they wed.

Jenna heard a faint click, followed by the distant rumble of a pump. She'd give it a few minutes to fill the holding tank before she tested the faucet again.

Abe came into the kitchen, wiping dusty spider webs off the brim of his hat set on his black hair. She looked away, wishing she hadn't noticed how the clumsy kid had become such a good-looking man. Not that how he looked mattered. He was Amish and rooted in Sweetwater. She was neither Amish nor planning to stay here. There were some avenues she hadn't explored that could lead to her working on a street patrol instead of behind a desk. She wasn't ready to let go of her chance to continue having a law enforcement career.

"All set." He closed the cellar door with his left hand. Wasn't he right-handed? She would have noticed if he were left-handed because her father, Nevin Shetler, had been. Her mother never talked about him, so Jenna had depended on *Grossmammi* Dinah to tell her about the man who'd been killed while riding a motorcycle when Jenna was two.

"Thanks, and thanks for bringing my bags in." She hoped he'd take her words as a hint to leave.

He didn't. Resting one hand on the butcher block counter *Grossmammi* Dinah had kept oiled to a sheen, he asked, "Are you staying here for six weeks?"

"That's the plan."

"To get the letters Dinah left behind?"

"Yes, and follow the instructions in them. I explained this outside."

He took off his straw hat. "It's so—so—"

"Ridiculous? Weird? Unheard of? Trust me," she said with a wry smile, "I've thought of every possible description since Ken told me about the will." She coughed again. "Let me see if there's water now."

He stepped aside as she took a plastic glass from the cupboard next to the sink. She turned the water on.

A loud retort came from the faucet, which jumped as if it were alive. More thuds rattled the water lines in the wall and below them in the cellar.

A howl came from the front of the house. She shrieked as she flung the glass in the sink and whirled so fast she almost tumbled to the floor. She slammed into Abe, shoving him into a corner, planting herself in front of him.

He drew in a breath to speak, but went silent as a brown-and-black blur burst through the door. Brown and black and with bared white teeth. Buddy growled, his hackles raised like a punk hairdo.

Jenna's voice was low and steady. "It's okay, Buddy. Just the faucet." She looked over her shoulder at the wide-eyed man behind her. "Just Abe. Just the faucet and just Abe."

The dog dropped to the floor, trembling. Jenna inched toward him, crooning the words over and over. When Abe took a step forward, she motioned him back.

She knelt, smoothing the dog's fur. "Buddy. Just the faucet and just Abe."

The dog gazed at her, then relaxed. She held back tears from her eyes, not wanting to upset him further. She petted him and told him what a good boy he was. When the dog rolled to let her rub his chest, she heard Abe release the breath she guessed he'd been holding since her partner raced into the room.

Jenna used the table to lever herself up. Buddy jumped to his three feet, too.

"What was *that*?" Abe asked. "He was about to attack and now acts like a puppy."

"Buddy doesn't like loud noises." How could she explain Buddy's PTSD was triggered by some sounds and her PTSD by others? Her own memories of odors and pain and screams and the hard floor beneath her cheek and Buddy's body so still in her arms erupted through her head, dragging a raging headache in their wake. She kept her head high so Abe couldn't guess how she was fighting an invisible battle for her sanity. There was no way he'd understand a sound could recreate odors of burnt clothing and spent explosives. He only knew the safe, quiet life of a plain person.

The serrated fingers of panic climbed her throat. *No time-out now,* she repeated mentally, as if she had control over the episodes. She didn't, but sometimes the mantra staved one off.

Jenna released her breath as the tentacles receded. She patted her partner's side. "It's okay, Buddy."

As if nothing had happened, the dog trotted back into the dining room to discover any other interesting scents that might be there.

Abe relaxed when Buddy left. She wanted to ask him if he disliked all dogs or only Buddy, but didn't when he gestured toward the yard. "I should…"

"Go ahead. I'm sure you want to check on your kids "

"They're my sister and brother, not my kids. They're five years old."

A peculiar warmth flickered inside her when he confirmed he was single, but she ignored it. She already knew the cost of having feelings toward Abe. She'd learned that lesson the last summer she'd come to Sweetwater. She'd had a crush on him. He'd acted as if she were silly.

He'd been right. That had been the first time she'd made a mistake in picking a guy, but not the last.

Jenna kept her tone light. "My only kid is Buddy. He's five years old, too."

"So no human kids?"

She shook her head. "No. Before you give me the full third degree, no husband or boyfriend."

"I wasn't going to ask that. Your life is none of my business."

And his was none of hers. He hadn't said that, but it was implied. She was grateful. If they didn't talk about their pasts, she could avoid explaining how her two-year relationship with her ex—Richard Benoist—had imploded after the bomb that took her lower leg.

She was eager to change the subject because she'd embarrassed herself enough already. "Abe, I need to go through the mail and see if the first of *Grossmammi* Dinah's letters is here. If you'll excuse me…"

"Your father's cousin… Or is Daryl his second cousin or—"

"Just call him my cousin. I think he's my first cousin once removed or something like that."

"Okay. *Your* cousin and his wife won't be the only ones curious about what's going to happen with the farm."

"You don't have to remind me. Anyone's business in Sweetwater is everyone's. *Grossmammi* Dinah said that once a week."

He looked at the table. "If you don't mind, can I stay to see if you've gotten the first letter?"

Jenna sorted through the mail. *Grossmammi* Dinah should have been there to open her own mail. The pain that had flooded Jenna when she stepped out of the truck and faced her grandmother's house threatened to overwhelm her again.

The mail was junk and sales flyers except for two letters. She recognized the name of a friend *Grossmammi* Dinah had been corresponding with for years. The return address on the other envelope was topped by the law firm's logo. The sedate, but elegant, lettering suggested long-standing trustworthiness. Ken had given off that vibe in his office…until he'd begun to talk about her grandmother's odd will. Then he'd been as uncomfortable as she'd been the first time she was sent to the principal's office.

"Here we go." She held up the envelope. "Letter number one."

Abe hesitated, then asked, "Are you going to open it?"

It was her turn to falter. She didn't want him looking over her shoulder while she read what *Grossmammi* Dinah had written. It'd be better if there were no witnesses if she dissolved into tears.

"Maybe I should unpack first." She hated when people equivocated. Now she was doing it. "You know how *Grossmammi* Dinah wanted me settled in straightaway. That's the word she always used. Straightaway." She was babbling but she couldn't help herself. "If you'll excuse me, I should—"

"Are you going to pretend nothing's changed?" His voice was colder than she'd ever heard it…except one time. It'd been the summer he'd broken her trusting heart.

She wasn't that foolish girl any longer. She'd had some

tough lessons. Lifting her chin, she paid no attention to the pain clamping around her head. "I'm not pretending anything, Abe Bontranger. I gave that up years ago. Remember? You told me only stupid people believe in fairy tales."

Abe gripped a kitchen chair, not wanting Jenna to see how her words made him recoil from the memory of how cruel he'd been. He couldn't remember why he'd told her such a thing, but he'd never forgotten her shocked face.

Had it been because she'd annoyed him by insisting she play football with him and his friends? Those games had started out as touch football but devolved into tackling. When they were little kids, she'd been able to hold her own, but then he and his friends had grown taller and stronger. He'd given in and let her play, hoping it would teach her a lesson. He'd been sure she'd learned not to ask to join in again because she'd gone home with two skinned knees, a bloody nose and a black eye. She'd returned the next day, ready to play. It had been his first lesson in what strength was. It was also the reason he hadn't been surprised when he heard she'd become a cop. She'd always gone where the bravest angel would have feared to tread.

He forced his eyes not to shift toward her left leg again. He recalled hearing a year or so ago about a K-9 team in Philadelphia being injured while trying to find a bomb, but he'd never heard names. It had barely caught his attention. Had that story been about her and Buddy?

He thought of how she'd run and jumped and climbed trees. Now she had to consider each step she took. It seemed so cruel. He didn't like to question God, but he wanted to shout, *Why, Lord, why?*

"I'm sorry," he said. "I was a thoughtless kid."

"Weren't we all?" Jenna sighed. "I guess it's ludicrous to put off reading this." She looked at the envelope. "What did you write about first, *Grossmammi* Dinah? Is it about the house or the farm?"

Had a fist struck him in the gut? Daryl had told him multiple times Dinah had assured the Rickaboughs the farm would be theirs. Would Jenna contest the will? He'd spent more time with Dinah than her family had. He listened to her stories about when she first came to the farm with her husband, who'd died more than thirty-five years ago. She'd had been delighted when Abe had begun repairing the buildings.

"There's only one way to find out what's in there," he said. "Open it."

She did and pulled out a single bright pink page. As she unfolded it, Abe could see Dinah's handwriting. He grinned. Dinah wouldn't have allowed her final wishes to be typed on an unfeeling computer.

"Ready?" Jenna asked.

If it'd been anyone else, he would have said she was nervous. Not Jenna. He hoped he could draw on some of her serenity. "Ready."

"My dearest Jenna,
"Don't weep for me. It's my time, and God is gut to bring me home to be with your *grossdawdi*. When you read this, I shall be free from my earthly worries. Who knows? Maybe, even as you're reading this, I'll be getting a fitting for a pair of wings. You know how I like to have everything just right."

Jenna paused to wipe away a tear, but she was smiling. He realized he was, too. Trust Dinah to give them a chuckle even after her death.

Lifting the page again, she went on:

"Abe will make sure the animals are taken care of, but remind him Maude and Maeve should get treats only once a week. They'll try to convince him to give them more."

Jenna's forehead ruffled. "Who are Maude and Maeve?"

"Dinah's two Highland cows. They're partial to apples." He chuckled. "They act like calves when they see me coming with treats."

"*Grossmammi* Dinah loved her animals."

"She did because they were, for her, part of her family."

More tears welled from the corners of her eyes, but she began to read again before he could say he was sorry for making her cry.

> "As I'm sure Ken has explained, I've made series of bequests. Six in all. You'll receive a letter weekly at the farm. Try to complete the instructions in one before the next arrives."

He arched his brows as Jenna wiped away tears. "Dinah trusts you."

"She does—did."

"I guess she remembered how focused on details you are."

Instead of the quick retort he'd expected, she flinched so hard her hands trembled. What had he said wrong? He'd meant his words as a compliment. Instead she acted as if he'd accused her of some heinous crime.

Her voice shook as she continued:

> "This first week will be easy. I want you to take the nine-patch quilt and give it to the Glicks. I know you may get some back talk, but they'll be grateful to have that old quilt. Thank you, my dear girl. If you have questions, you know where you can turn for help. If you need a hint, look in the barn. You'll find help there."

"Is she talking about Daryl?" Jenna looked up while folding the letter and slipping it into the envelope.

"He's not over here very often."

She frowned. "So *Grossmammi* Dinah means you?"

"It sounds like it, though I'm not sure how I'm to help."

"Can you tell me what a nine-patch quilt is? *Grossmammi* Dinah's got a lot of quilts around here. As to the Glicks, which Glicks? There's got to be more than one Glick family around Sweetwater."

"Almost a dozen."

"If this is an 'easy' bequest, I don't want to think about the others." Her shrug made her blond curls dance. "I've got a week to figure it out, right?"

"I can help right now." He crooked his finger. "Come to the living room."

As he led the way, he glanced toward the dining room, but her dog wasn't in there. Where had it gone? He caught the motion of a wagging tail as the German shepherd went upstairs, climbing as if it had four legs. It slowed so Jenna could reach between the spindles to pat its head. Again he suppressed his shudder.

He paused by the living room's hearth. Above it hung an old quilt. It was a series of red-and-green blocks set in a black background. Each block was a different design.

"This is a nine-patch quilt." He pointed out the pattern. "See? The blocks are made up of nine different smaller blocks."

"*A* nine-patch quilt? Could there be others?"

"I don't know, but Dinah said this one is special. It was…" He paused at the sound of an excited squeal and looked out the window. Zoe was lying on her belly across the tire while Zeke stood with his feet on either side of her. They were making the tire move, much to their obvious delight.

"They'll be okay."

"I just wanted to check."

"I get that." This time, her smile seemed more natural than any he'd seen since her arrival.

It reminded him of ones when her front teeth had been missing and others when braces had made smiling a chore. He had to wonder if anything of that young girl who'd found amazement and joy in the simplest things was left in her.

Before he could halt himself, he blurted, "What happened to you?"

"Buddy and I are—we were—a K-9 bomb-sniffing team." Warmth left her voice. "We found a lot of bombs, but we didn't find that last one in time."

"God was with you that day."

She arched her brows. "If you say so."

"You don't believe in God?"

"I do believe in Him."

"Then believe He was with you that day. You're alive, not dead."

The wrong thing to say when her *grossmammi* had just passed. The very worst thing, he realized when tears swelled in her eyes, answering his question.

Ja, the young, vulnerable girl he'd known was still inside her.

Chapter Three

Morning, four days later, began at the Bontranger house as it always did. Abe, after doing the morning milking at Dinah's farm, helped one of his sisters make breakfast while their *daed* and *mamm* spent the whole meal on their phones, arranging for building supplies and closing deals. He wondered when they'd last noticed what was put in front of them to eat. Some mornings, they paused long enough to give their *kinder* a reminder of the tasks for that day. Today they'd been on their phones before they arrived at the table and they were still on them when they left for their offices across the road.

The rest of the family had learned to live around the business. Breakfast was served, silent grace was shared and then they ate, also in silence. As soon as *Daed* and *Mamm* left the kitchen, a babble began. Abe and his siblings enjoyed each other's company before heading off for work or school or, for the twins, being watched by an older brother or sister. That older sibling was Abe now that school was out and the others had jobs in the family business or in Sweetwater.

The kitchen became quiet again as everybody began to leave. He gathered the dirty dishes and put them by the sink where his sixteen-year-old sister, Sara Beth, was washing them. She worked at an ice cream shop in Sweetwater four days a week. The hair beneath her heart-shaped *kapp* was as black as her apron.

As he turned to head out himself, she said, "Abe, I need to talk with you."

"Sure." Abe realized he hadn't finished his *kaffi*. He downed the last of it in one gulp. Going to the sink, he lowered the cup into suds. "About what?"

She didn't meet his eyes. Her lashes were dark against her too-pale face.

"Are you feeling okay?" he asked, wishing again—as he had for more times than he could count—that his six sisters and four brothers would go to *Daed* and *Mamm* with their problems instead of to him. "Do you need me to contact the Sweet Shop and let them know you are sick? There's a phone in the barn at Dinah's." He knew *Daed* and *Mamm* would be monopolizing the phones in the Barnwood Mills office.

"Abe, I'm not sick." Her face was so ashen it could have been made of the storm clouds hanging over the house. With her eyes downcast, she whispered, "I think I'm pregnant."

"You're pregnant?" He stared at his sister who seemed like a *kind* to him, as impetuous and fun-loving as the twins. "Are you sure?"

"Yes." A single tear rolled down her cheek.

"Have you seen a *doktor*?"

She shook her head. "I took a pregnancy test. Don't worry. I didn't buy the test in Sweetwater. I went into Ocean City. Nobody knows us there."

He didn't say an Amish girl in Ocean City would have caught a lot of attention, especially one buying a pregnancy test. "Was the test positive?"

"I think so."

He frowned. "Think so? You either are pregnant or you aren't, ain't so?"

She shrugged. He resisted insisting she meet his eyes. That wouldn't get him anywhere with Sara Beth. She could be as stubborn as...well, as stubborn as Jenna Rose Shetler.

Shoving Dinah's *kins-kind* out of his thoughts wasn't easy. "Sara Beth, you need to be sure. One way or the other."

"Don't tell *Mamm* and *Daed* until I'm sure. Please." Another tear tumbled. "I just needed to tell someone."

"I know." He wanted to hug her, but she wasn't a *kind* with a skinned knee. "How long until you're sure?"

"I should know within a month." She looked at him with dark gray eyes so much like his own. "Rhetta had a scare in the spring. The test said she was pregnant, but it turned out when she took a second one a few weeks later, she wasn't." She took a deep breath. "I may not be either."

"If there's a chance you're pregnant—"

"Of course, there's a chance, Abe. I wouldn't have taken the test otherwise."

"Have you told Kenny?"

She flushed, and he wondered why she'd thought he didn't know she'd been walking out with Kenny Nolt. "No."

"When are you planning on telling him?"

"When I know for sure. Why would I tell him before that?"

He wanted to ask why she'd told *him* before she was certain she was pregnant, but already knew the answer. He'd been *mamm* and *daed* to his siblings. It wasn't a position he'd ever wanted, but he'd never figured out a way to let it go.

Before she left for work at the ice cream shop, Abe gave her a hug. After a month, he insisted, she must reveal her suspicions to her boyfriend and to their parents. She didn't want to agree, but did.

Abe's mind felt as if it were being whirled on a carnival ride as he went across the road to work in the production barn. Last week, he would have found a haven at Dinah's farm where he could be alone with his thoughts and figure out what to do. That wasn't a sanctuary for him any longer. Not while Jenna Rose was there.

An hour later, when a buggy pulled to a stop in front of the open-ended barn, Abe's thoughts were still as jumpy as oil on a heated pan. The driver was Elden Bing. Their bishop was a large man with a huge, black beard. When he stepped out and called to Abe, his face was grim. Had he heard rumors that Sara Beth was pregnant?

"*Gute mariye.*" Abe stopped sweeping sawdust from under the circular saw that sliced debarked logs into boards.

"Do you have a minute, Abe?"

"*Ja.*" He leaned the broom on the wall, then walked toward the bishop.

The tall sign announcing Barnwood Mills was open six days a week soared over the trees. It had been set so the words could be read on the other side of the Pocomoke River. In the morning, its shadow darkened everything between the production buildings and the family's house. Now, the shadow was retreating toward the base of the sign, leaving the buggy in the sunlight.

"Hot one, ain't so?" The bishop wiped his brow.

"Too hot for June." Abe waited, knowing Elden hadn't driven two miles to talk about the weather.

"Did you hear about the chickens over at the Rodgers' farm?"

"The ones that got out?"

"The ones that were *let* out."

Abe arched a brow. Chickens were the way most farm families around Sweetwater made their living. They were sold to processing plants in Maryland, Delaware and Pennsylvania. Allowing the chickens to get out meant a big loss to the farmers. Plus, there was the chance a bird that got out could infect the whole flock with avian flu.

"I'm assuming it wasn't an accident," Abe said.

"It was mischief pure and simple. Graffiti sprayed on the barn and birds scattered." Elden frowned. "Fingers are being pointed at our kids because what look like the marks made by buggy wheels were found."

"Plain folks work at the Rodgers' farm."

"But they don't leave their buggies where these marks were discovered." The bishop pulled off his straw hat. "That's why I came to see you. You've done some work with the running-around groups, ain't so?"

"*Ja*." He had been part of one group of teens during his *rumspringa*, but had seldom attended because he was too busy at home. He'd become more involved as a chaperone when his siblings were old enough to join.

There were a variety of running-around groups in the community. Most plain teens joined to spend time with friends and meet a future spouse. Others had no interest in a taffy pull or a singing. They were the kids who looked for ways to make mischief.

"The *Englischers* have groups for what they call 'troubled teens.' I think we should have one of those, too." Elden's face remained stern. "You'd be the best person to lead it, Abe. You've done a *gut* job with your brothers and sisters, so maybe you can help these kids who are loitering on the edge of the law. You could keep them from tumbling over that edge."

The bishop wasn't a man who took no for an answer, so Abe didn't try. He agreed to hold a meeting for the teens Elden and the other ordained men chose. He had to wonder how he could help other teens when he'd failed his own sister.

The nine-patch quilt was draped over the sofa, reminding Jenna she was no closer to getting it to the person *Grossmammi* Dinah wanted to have it than when she'd opened the envelope four days ago.

I want you to take the nine-patch quilt and give it to the Glicks. I know you may get some back talk, but they'll be grateful to have that old quilt.

By now, she'd read and reread the words in *Grossmammi* Dinah's letter. She'd perused the Amish directory listing the community members' addresses in Sweetwater and nearby towns. She'd seen plenty of Glicks, too many to contact. Or so she'd thought that first day. Now she realized if she'd started then, she might already have the answer.

"Too late for that now, Buddy." She spread peanut butter on a piece of naan bread. He watched every motion she made as if his gaze alone could persuade her to share one of his favorite treats. Even after so many years on her own, her culinary skills didn't extend much beyond making sandwiches and salads. She'd often depended on delivery. That had become even more common after Richard had left, breaking off their engagement.

She forced cheerfulness into her voice. "Buddy, I haven't forgotten you."

When she'd filled his toy with peanut butter and rolled it across the floor, he took off after it as if he had four legs. She left him licking the bright yellow toy while she sat at the table and picked up her sandwich. Staring at it, she sighed. *Grossmammi* Dinah had made her peanut butter sandwiches day after day each summer.

How she longed to hear her grandmother call her name across the fields! She would have been happy even to sit and hold *Grossmammi* Dinah's yarn while the older woman rolled it into a ball, though it had been a trial to remain still for so long when she was small.

A motion outside caught her eye. Was it Abe? Since her arrival on the farm, she'd seen Abe doing chores, but he hadn't come to the house. She'd been relieved the first couple of days. She'd needed time to focus on the house. She'd started by airing the rooms and making lists of work that should be done before the house was sold.

By yesterday, Jenna had been going stir-crazy. Flowers

bloomed in the yard, but she didn't cut any, not sure if doing so would keep them from blossoming again. She'd gone to see the animals, but they'd ignored her once they realized she wasn't bringing food. The birds' songs, which had delighted her when she first got to the farm, seemed to be mocking her as she walked around the house, trying to figure out the meaning in the first letter. Long walks with Buddy had been great until they went past the same houses on every trip.

Jenna headed toward Abe, who was working near the barn, before she gave herself a chance to think of the reasons she shouldn't. Maybe he'd solved the mystery of the quilt's new owner. There were only three days left. She owed *Grossmammi* Dinah so much and taking care of the weird will was a small way to repay her.

"Abe?"

He faced her. Why did smiling look so tough for him? Was he still upset over Buddy's reaction when the faucet blew out the air in the line? Or maybe he was annoyed she'd come to the farm. His welcome had been sparse and cool.

Too bad, she wanted to tell him. She needed his help on her grandmother's behalf. If for no other reason than that, he should help her. Though *Grossmammi* Dinah hadn't talked about others often, she'd mentioned how heavy a load Abe carried. She hadn't said anything else. She hadn't needed to. Everyone in Sweetwater knew how Abe's parents spent more time with their business than their children.

"How are you doing?" she asked when he didn't answer.

"I'm fine."

If he were fine, she was an elephant. "I was wondering if you had any ideas about—"

"Jenna, I need to talk to you about something."

"All right." She clasped her hands behind her and raised her chin so she could meet his eyes.

They shifted away. Shame. She couldn't fail to recognize

it, because shame was an emotion she'd seen often on people she'd arrested...and in her own mirror.

He cleared his throat. "I should have mentioned this the day you got here. I've got an agreement with the Rickaboughs to buy this place after they inherit it."

"If they inherit the farm."

"They will. Daryl told me Dinah mentioned the disposition of her property about two years ago. He knew I was looking for a place of my own, so I've been milking and tending the animals as well as doing handyman jobs around the farm. The value of my work is going against my down payment."

"A cozy arrangement, and you had it before *Grossmammi* Dinah died?"

He had the decency to flush at her cold words. "She was pleased when I began fixing up the barns."

"What a creepy arrangement!" She rolled her eyes. "*Grossmammi* Dinah used to say Daryl liked to chase people with snakes and bugs."

"He seems all right now...other than when he got upset the day you arrived." Abe hadn't changed in one way. He saw the best in everyone.

She wished she could be that way, but no cop would last long if she believed everyone had goodness at heart. "The whole arrangement is ghoulish."

"When I hear myself talking about it, I've got to agree. The arrangement has been sensible, and I'm surprised Dinah didn't tell you I've been working here."

"I haven't been able to get out a lot in the past year, so I didn't get a chance to talk to her about much." She tried not to squirm as she thought of how seldom she'd visited her grandmother even before the bomb exploded.

"Oh." He stared at her left leg for a long minute. "I wanted you to know about the arrangement. You've had enough surprises. You never liked surprises."

"I don't." She gave him a smile as fake as his. "Proud member of 'My Way or the Highway Anonymous.' That's why I hate that I haven't figured out the first letter from *Grossmammi* Dinah."

"What did it say again?"

"The pertinent part is: 'I want you to take the nine-patch quilt and give it to the Glicks. I know you may get some back talk, but they'll be grateful to have that old quilt.'"

He grinned. "I think I know what she meant. Dinah said Glicks and something about talking back, but they'd like having the quilt. Dinah wants the quilt to go to Gaylord Glick's wife."

"Why?"

"Back talk. It's a synonym for sass, right?"

She nodded, frowning. "So?"

"Gaylord's wife's name is Sass."

"*Sass* Glick? An Amish woman has a name like that?"

He chuckled. "Her real name is Sallie, and I'm not sure how she got the nickname. The connection makes sense to me because she's the person everyone goes to in order to find out about old quilts."

"Thanks, Abe. I wouldn't have figured it out alone." She smiled as she fished in the pocket of her jeans and pulled out the keys to her truck. "Let me get her address, and I'll drop off the quilt. One letter down, five to go."

Stepping in front of her, he said, "You don't need to look it up. I know it."

"So tell me."

"No. I'm coming with you. It's been a long time since you've been on the roads around here, and it's easy to get turned around. I'll go with you if…"

"If what?"

"Are you planning on taking your dog?" Again his smile disappeared.

She put her hands on her hips and met his gaze. "I don't remember you not liking dogs."

"It's not about liking. It's about not trusting." He held out his right hand.

She gasped when she saw the thick ropy scars by his two outer fingers.

"That's what happened," he said, "the last time I trusted a dog."

"Buddy won't attack you. Not unless I ordered him to."

He drew in a deep breath, then released it. "Don't expect us to be friends."

"I'm not my grandmother. I'm not into matchmaking."

"Glad to hear that." Abe's shoulders sagged. "Sorry to snap at you. I've got a lot on my mind, Jenna Rose."

"I told you I'm Jenna now." She walked toward the truck.

He kept pace with her. "I'll try to remember that, but, like I said, I've got a bunch of things on my mind right now." He put a hand on the truck's hood. "In fact, if you're okay with it, I've got something I'd like your opinion on."

"What's that?"

"Let's talk in the truck on our way to the Glicks'. It's not far, and—"

"Yikes! I can't give anyone a quilt I don't have with me. Just a sec."

Jenna hurried at her best speed inside and got the old quilt. She held it with care as she paused long enough to tell Buddy to come with her.

He wagged his tail and jumped to his feet, leaving his favorite treat for later.

Jenna paused by the front door. Its glass framed the white truck under the wide branches of the maple tree and the man beside it. Abe hadn't changed that much, and neither had her ridiculous heart, which beat a little harder when she looked at his broad shoulders and remembered her arms around them as they raced against their friends with him carrying her on his back.

Had she lost her mind? How far away was Sass Glick's house? *Not far* could have a lot of different definitions. However long the trip took, she'd be in her truck close to Abe as she hadn't since the night she'd told him she loved him…and he'd laughed in her face.

Now her grandmother's will and his plans to buy the farm had thrown them together once more. She reached for the knob.

Grossmammi *Dinah, what were you thinking when you set up this will?*

Chapter Four

The Glick house was on the edge of the village of Sweetwater. It was set back from the road just like *Grossmammi* Dinah's farm. Flowers blossomed in neat precision in the front yard. Behind the house, a garden plot claimed most of the space. Some plants were already swelling with leaves while others weren't much more than green fuzz against the turned ground. Beyond the house were two long barns with giant fans at the ends.

Commercial chicken houses, Jenna knew. Farms around Sweetwater raised chickens for eggs or meat while other farmers cultivated corn and soybeans to feed the chickens.

Though Abe had said he had something on his mind he wanted to discuss, he didn't say much on the way to the Glicks'. He asked about her sister, whom he'd never met because Susan hadn't come to Sweetwater, and the rest of her family. She didn't mention she hadn't spoken to her own sister in almost four years.

She noticed him eyeing Buddy in the back seat, but he didn't say anything. Was he thinking as she was about the other letters attached to the will? The first had taken her almost a whole week to decipher…assuming they'd accurately guessed its meaning. Five more to come, and *Grossmammi* Dinah had said this first one was an easy one.

She wanted to groan, but swallowed her annoyance. She adored her grandmother; yet this incomprehensible will was beyond bizarre. Why hadn't *Grossmammi* Dinah just written a list of beneficiaries and what items she wanted them to have…like everyone else in the world did?

One thing was certain. There *was* an answer. Her grandmother always had a reason for everything she did.

With a glance toward where Abe was looking out the passenger window, she wondered if she should share the other letters with him. Maybe with his Amish upbringing, he'd understand what her grandmother meant. His head swiveled toward her, and she quickly focused her own gaze on the curving country road. Keeping an invisible guardrail between them would be smart.

She stopped her truck behind the house where a buggy and an open cart were parked. Overhead, on a long pulley line, laundered clothing flapped in the strong breeze off the ocean.

Abe settled his straw hat on his head as he stepped from the truck. Not waiting for her and Buddy, he strode toward the back door where a basket waited for the clothes once they were dry and folded.

Jenna got out from behind the wheel. She'd thought Abe would offer to carry the bulky quilt, then wondered if he wanted to give her the honor of handing over her grandmother's bequest. That was kind of him, but she would have appreciated him asking.

You would have turned him down if he asked, her conscience nagged her. *You're too stubborn to let someone help. Before and now.*

She ignored that small voice as she reached the back door just as a woman came out.

"Abe Bontranger!" The Amish woman smiled. "What brings you here today?"

"Sass, do you remember Dinah's *kins-kind*?"

"Little Jenna Rose?" Her smile turned toward Jenna and Buddy.

Sass Glick was a short, spare woman from the top of her heart-shaped *kapp* to the bottom of her black sneakers. Her face was narrow, and her shoulder bones were visible beneath her dark cranberry dress. Even her graying hair was thinning at its center from years of being pulled into a bun. Yet when she smiled, there was something so genuine, so kind, in her expression.

"That's me." Jenna didn't bother to say—yet again—she'd dropped the "Rose" when she went to high school.

"Oh, my dear *kind*." Sass swooped in to give Jenna a big hug, compressing the quilt between them.

Buddy stiffened. "Buddy, just Sass." She quickly explained how Buddy had been her K-9 partner and was protective of her.

"I'm glad you've got someone to watch over you." Sass's smile faded. "I'm so sorry about the passing of your *gross-mammi*. Dinah was one of a kind, and we were blessed to have known her."

"We were." She was happy to agree.

"*Komm* in, so we can talk without towels thumping Abe around the ears. That's what you get for being so tall, Abe."

"That's what I get," he replied, "because you're so short you need to have this end of the line close to the ground."

"True, true." With a laugh, she opened the door.

Jenna followed the others inside a kitchen with beautifully made cupboards that would have been the envy of any high-end home in Philadelphia. Simple, air-driven appliances sat on the counter along with several vases of flowers. The walls were light blue, and the appliances a simple white except for a black wood stove that heated the space during the cold, damp winter days. Hardwood floors shone in the sunshine coming through the windows that were decorated with white lower panels. A large table in the middle of the room served as prep space as well because a bowl with flour sat amidst containers of eggs and milk.

She told Buddy to lie down, gave him a treat and promised another if he'd stay put. He obeyed, but his eyes scanned the room, and his nose twitched as he took in the scents around them.

Sass pulled out a chair. "Do you want to put that quilt here?"

"Thank you." Jenna was glad to set the bulky quilt down. "I don't know if you've heard *Grossmammi* Dinah made me executor of her will."

"I'm not surprised. She has always said you have an extraordinary amount of common sense."

Jenna didn't dare to look in Abe's direction to see his reaction to Sass's words. He never had thought she had a lick of common sense. She couldn't have been described as cautious when she was young. She'd been the first to jump into a pond or climb a tree, but she wasn't that little girl any longer. She wouldn't have lasted long patrolling city streets if she hadn't learned to be careful and consider every possibility before she acted.

So why had *Grossmammi* Dinah thought she was sensible? How Jenna wished she could ask her grandmother that as well as so many other things. A wave of grief threatened to smother her.

Swallowing hard, she squared her shoulders and blinked back tears she refused to let fall. She put her hand on the quilt on the chair. "Sass, my grandmother wanted you to have this."

"This quilt?" Sass's hushed voice suggested that *Grossmammi* Dinah had given her the older woman's most precious possession. "For me? I can't believe it."

"Well, believe it." Abe chuckled.

"It's her oldest quilt. The only one she bought instead of making."

"I didn't know that." Jenna was astonished. "I thought she made all the quilts in the house."

"All but this one." Sass ran her fingers over the fabric in awe. "It has to be more than one hundred sixty years old."

She opened a door and went into a room where Jenna caught a glimpse of a sewing machine connected to what appeared to be a car battery. *Grossmammi* Dinah had powered her own sewing machine the same way.

Sass returned with a large box lined with fabric. "For now, I'm putting it in an acid-free box with this muslin around it. That will protect it until I can clean and examine it." She put the lid on the box and splayed her hands across the top. "Jenna Rose, this means so much to me. I know you know what a *wunderbaar* woman your *grossmammi* was. I'm glad because I don't have the words to express what this means to me. Not just for the quilt, but that she remembered how much I enjoyed seeing it at her house."

"Dinah seldom forgot anything," Abe said before Jenna could reply. "Not the *gut* or the bad." He chuckled. "Or the naughty."

They laughed, and the yearning to weep swept Jenna again. It'd been such a short time since her grandmother's passing. Her hope that she had her emotions under control had been premature.

Sass urged Jenna to return after the quilt was refreshed. As she walked with them to the door, Sass asked, "Are the old, torn quilts still in a trunk in the attic?"

"I don't know. I haven't gone up there yet."

"Dinah couldn't bear to part with them, even though most are as thin as a single sheet. She planned to repair them." Sass lowered her eyes. "I hope you won't think I'm pushy, but I'd be glad to take them and fix the ones that can be fixed. I know you're a police officer now, Jenna Rose."

"I am." She steeled herself for what Sass might say next because she was too aware of how the plain people considered such a job not one they'd want any member of their family, no matter which side of the fence they stood on, to have.

"That's why I feel it's God working through us for me to

ask you to let me take the quilts. I'll sew them together to be used as comforters for the police and other first responders to give to people who've suffered trauma."

Jenna nodded, those bothersome tears making a reappearance. She recalled her grandmother mentioning the quilts and how during one of Jenna's infrequent visits she wanted to discuss how to put them to the best possible use. Had she intended to do as Sass was proposing? Jenna would never know, because she'd changed the subject. *Grossmammi* Dinah had wanted Jenna to take custody of the ruined quilts, something she had no room for in her cramped apartment. Just the thought of how her ex, Richard, would have reacted with disgust at frayed and dusty quilts had compelled Jenna to say no. Now she had to wonder if her grandmother had wanted to offer them for use in Jenna's precinct. It would have been an amazing gift, and Jenna had denied *Grossmammi* Dinah the chance to offer it.

She brushed tears away in what she hoped would look like a casual motion. "That would be a great idea, Sass."

"The rest of them, the ones that can't be fully repaired, can be used when the police find abused animals."

"Abused animals?"

Sass and Abe nodded at the same time before Sass said, "Word is the police are close to finding some abused animals. Once they do, they'll turn them over to the country rescue volunteers. I've gathered my ripped quilts and old blankets and taken them to the animal rescue league. If you find more, I'm sure they'd be happy to get them. That's what your *grossmammi* would have wanted."

"Thank you for letting me know that." Jenna motioned for Buddy to follow her as she left before she couldn't restrain her tears any longer.

Abe was astonished Jenna was able to keep from asking the questions in her tear-filled eyes while they went to the truck.

Her whole demeanor had changed when Sass mentioned mistreated animals. He wasn't surprised. He'd seen how much she treasured her dog.

As for him, he would have been happy if she put the German shepherd in the cargo bed instead of letting the big dog breathe on him, a constant reminder of how close Buddy stood. The dog hadn't shown any signs of aggression, but neither had the dog that had maimed Abe's hand.

Ignoring the dog wasn't easy until Jenna asked, "What did she mean about abused animals?"

He gripped the door handle as the truck bounced over a pair of potholes. "There have been rumors spreading around town for a while about a puppy mill."

Her voice became hard. "I've heard about them in Pennsylvania. Breeders who breed their dogs too often and make them live in intolerable conditions. Breeders who don't care if their dogs die because they've got more. Breeders who sell sick and dying puppies to middlemen who peddle them to unscrupulous pet stores. We would hear reports out of rural counties about raids where hundreds of dogs were rescued. I didn't know there were any puppy mills in Sweetwater."

"My guess is that some breeders got tired of the inspections in Pennsylvania and moved their facilities here. They're supposed to get a license to raise dogs, but they go underground. Nobody asks questions, and dogs suffer."

"As well as the families who adopt the dogs, expecting to get a healthy puppy." She clenched her hands on the wheel. "Why don't the animal welfare people close them down?"

"They have to find them first. These breeders are clever. They may disguise their puppy mill with selling a few dogs that are healthy, or they may try raising other animals to hide their real business. The Amish have gotten a bad reputation as uncaring breeders, but I can assure you nobody in the districts around here is breeding dogs." He chuckled, but with little humor. "Dogs and chickens aren't a great mix. Chickens run, and dogs like to chase them."

She remained somber. "Not if the dogs are kept in cages and never let out. It makes me sick to think of them living in such conditions. Buddy was a rescue, but he didn't come from a puppy mill. His trainer mentioned that someone in the family that originally adopted him developed an allergy to dogs, and they donated him for training. It must have broken his heart to lose his family."

"He came to you."

"That didn't turn out so well for him, did it?"

"Is that how you see it? I see a dog that adores you and wants to spend every minute with you. Shouldn't you be thanking God your partner is alive?"

"It's difficult because he did his job."

"You didn't?"

She pressed her lips together, and he knew he'd poked an unhealed wound. Though he was curious, he didn't push.

A full minute of silence hung in the truck's cab before she said, "I hope the rumor about puppy mills is just that. A rumor."

"Most rumors are."

She shifted the subject. "Thanks for coming with me to drop off the quilt, Abe. It was nice to see Sass's obvious love for quilts."

"Do you quilt?"

She laughed, sounding as she had when she was a *kind*. With unfettered delight. He was glad he'd helped her find a way to change from anger to *gut* humor.

Moments ago, she'd been encased in silence, draped in the invisible cloak of pain. When she replied, he understood her amusement.

"Abe, the domestic gene missed me. I can barely sew on a button. A quilt is way, way beyond me. I guess when my dad jumped the fence, he left those plain skills behind."

"Not all Amish women quilt. The ones in my family don't." He savored her profile as she navigated with ease through the traffic. "I've never seen my *mamm* with a needle and thread in her hand."

"That's because she's got a nail gun instead. I admire how your mother works side by side with your father, doing what he does without complaint."

"She tries to do her best."

Ja, *Mamm* had done well because her oldest *kinder* had taken over her role as a parent. While Abe had raised his siblings, Sara Beth had taught herself to cook and to clean their home. She must have learned to mend their clothing and taught their other sisters, too, though Abe couldn't remember seeing her do so. Probably because he was trying to keep up with the younger ones.

"You said you had something you wanted to discuss with me." Jenna glanced at him.

"I did."

"Did you change your mind?"

He shook his head and rested his elbow on the open window. "No, but I'm not sure how to ask what I need to ask."

"I've found the easiest way is to ask it. Tiptoeing around things confuses everyone."

"All right. Here it is. Do you remember Elden Bing?"

"Wasn't he the guy who was ordained as a minister the next to last summer I came here?"

"I'm surprised you remember because you didn't attend services often."

"Three-plus hours of sitting on a backless bench was torture. Recalling that got me through physical training at the police academy. Nothing our instructors threw at me could make me ache more than sitting so long with my feet dangling."

He smiled. "Your feet touched the floor by the time you were ten."

"Not until I was eleven, and it's my memory, so I'll tell the story, if you please." She hit the indicator to signal a right turn. "I remember *Grossmammi* Dinah was pleased Elden had been chosen by the lot."

"She was even more pleased, two years ago, when he became our bishop. The *Leit* has been as blessed with him as our bishop as they were when he was a minister."

"That's nice to hear." She pulled into the drive to Dinah's house. "Why are we talking about Elden Bing?"

"Because he's worried about our youth being involved in petty crimes."

She braked the truck to a smooth stop. "One thing I've learned is kids lose brain cells when they get together in groups. Things they would never do on their own seem like the best idea ever when they're with friends."

"He'd agree with you."

"And you?"

"And me what?"

"Do you agree?"

Instead of answering her question, he outlined what the bishop had asked him to do with the teens. "Will you help, Jenna? Hearing from a police officer about the trouble they could find themselves in might be a really *gut* thing."

She didn't answer as he reached for the handle to open the door, then paused while Buddy jumped out the other side and ran around the front of the truck. Feeling like a coward but not a fool, he waited until Jenna stepped out. Buddy focused his attention on her while Abe emerged and closed the door. The German shepherd glanced once in his direction, then acted as if he wasn't there.

Jenna straightened, and he was amazed again how steady she was on her prosthetic. "I'll be happy to come, Abe, but let's be honest. How much do you think kids who don't see what they're doing as real damage are going to listen to a police officer who's out of her jurisdiction?"

"The bishop is looking to reach kids who are in danger of becoming delinquents. If they can be convinced to stop before they get themselves into trouble they can't get out of, then we'll have succeeded."

"Let's see how it goes. If it looks as if I can make a difference in the next five weeks, then I'll be glad to help."

Something punched him in the gut as she spoke about leaving as soon as the terms of the will were fulfilled. Why would she remain in Sweetwater any longer? Her life and her work—which she seemed to love—were in Philadelphia. His life was here…just as it'd always been.

"Sounds *gut*." It didn't. His stomach cramped at the thought of saying goodbye to her, this time forever. "I'll let you know when the meeting is scheduled."

"Sounds good," she repeated to him. "Thanks again for going with me."

"My—"

She stumbled while turning. Catching her arm, he kept her on her feet, but froze at a threatening growl. The German shepherd was smaller than the dog that had attacked him, but Abe wasn't fooled. Buddy was solid muscle.

Releasing Jenna's arm, Abe took a step away. At the same time, she told the dog to lie down. She repeated the order, motioning with her hand.

Buddy dropped to the ground, but his gaze never moved from Abe.

"I'm sorry," Jenna said. "He's trained to protect me, and he doesn't know you."

If Abe had his way, he and the dog wouldn't cross paths again, but that wasn't realistic. "I've got chores around the farm."

"Buddy will ignore you then. It's when he believes I'm in

danger that he gets protective." She gave him a wobbly smile. "Thanks for keeping me from landing on my nose, but don't do that again."

"You expect me to let you fall on your face?"

"Yes." She walked toward the house, the dog at her side.

Abe took a deep breath and held it before turning in the opposite direction. Moments ago, he'd been upset because she was leaving at the end of six weeks. He'd changed his mind. The day she and her dog left couldn't come soon enough.

Chapter Five

"Abe, help me!"

"Abe, no, help me first!"

"Abe, do you know where my work boots are? Did Homer take them?"

"Abe, *komm* out to the workshop, son. I want your opinion on the new doors one of our vendors wants added to sheds."

"Abe…"

"Abe…"

Shaking his head, Abe strode along the asphalt road between his family's home and Dinah's farm. He should be accustomed to being pulled in ten different directions every morning, but today had been ludicrous. The twins seemed incapable of the slightest task, like putting apple butter on their toast. The two brothers between him and Sara Beth—Benuel and Homer—accused each other of making off with shirts, suspenders, boots and hats. He couldn't remember what his other siblings, the ones between Sara Beth and the twins, had asked him. By that time, *Daed* had stuck his head around the door and was calling to Abe.

In quick order, Abe had buttered the twins' toast, found his brothers' missing clothing—most of which had been tossed on the floor and got pushed under their beds—and resolved other issues that his ten siblings should have been able to handle on their own. He'd hurried out to the shop where *Daed* showed him the new design. It wouldn't work, they decided, because it hadn't taken into account how the doors needed to be balanced so they wouldn't swing shut.

The early morning humidity made him feel as if he stood in front of the woodstove when *Mamm* put the kettle on for tea. He'd seen two of his middle sisters trying to get his attention, but had headed toward the road. He needed to complete the barn chores, giving time for his head to stop throbbing with the echo of his name.

"Forgive me, God." He raised his eyes to the lush blue sky. "I should be grateful I can help my family. It's just that some days…"

He paused his prayer when he saw Jenna walking toward the road and the mailbox. Her German shepherd was keeping pace with her. Beyond her, the mail truck was pulling away. Abe paid it little attention as he took in the sight of her in a flowered, sleeveless shirt and a pair of khaki shorts. She wasn't bothered by anyone seeing her prosthesis. He almost told her that was how her *grossmammi* would have wanted her to act. Joys of life and its scars, visible and invisible, were part of the life God gave them.

"*Gute mariye*," Abe called.

Jenna reached into the mailbox. "That's 'good morning,' right?"

"*Ja.* You remember some *Deitsch*, ain't so?"

"Not much."

When her eyes shifted away from his, he couldn't help wondering if she was thinking of the night she'd told him she loved him. She'd learned how to say those words in *Deitsch*. He had thought she was joking when she told him, "*Ich liebe dich.*" He had laughed so hard he hadn't noticed the tears filling her eyes and splashing down her cheeks until it was too late. Because he hadn't believed she was serious, he'd found it impossible to apologize. Then she'd been gone…and he hadn't had a chance to talk to her for years.

Now it was too late. Maybe he was projecting his guilt on her, and she must have forgotten that evening because Dinah had mentioned Jenna had a fiancé. What had happened to him? She'd been quite emphatic the day she reappeared on the farm she didn't have a man in her life.

Something else he couldn't ask, so Abe looked at the page she held. "Is that the second letter from Dinah?"

"Yes. Right on schedule." She hesitated, then asked, "Would you mind me opening it now?"

"Go ahead."

"Good. I didn't think you'd mind. You've got more riding on these letters than I do."

An odd way of saying it. Why didn't she expect Dinah to leave her something special? Or had Dinah already given her that remembrance before her death? Jenna hadn't mentioned anything from her *grossmammi*, but then Jenna was being so much more closemouthed than she'd been as a kid. Back then, she'd spouted everything that came into her head.

Ich liebe dich, came the memory of her voice from where he'd buried it. *I love you.*

Abe watched as she opened the envelope. He understood why she didn't want to wait. She'd mentioned—more than once—that when she went into Sweetwater, everyone asked about *Grossmammi* Dinah's will. He'd faced the same questions. He couldn't miss the undercurrent of curiosity about who would inherit the farm, but Sweetwater residents seemed to accept that neither he nor Jenna knew any more than they did.

Everybody but the Rickaboughs. Daryl had come over every day for the past week on the flimsiest excuse and asked if there had been any news about the farm. Abe tried to have patience with him, but Daryl refused to believe Jenna was being honest with him.

"It's hot out here," Jenna said. "Hot and humid. Let's find some shade." She started toward the house, her dog close beside her.

"Okay if I tend to Maeve and Maude at the same time? I want to give them their treat."

"I'm glad they'll come for you. They ignore me."

He reached into his pocket and pulled out an apple he'd quartered at home. "This is why they like me. They'd spin on their back hooves to get some apple."

"I'll try to remember that if I ever need them to do a *pas de deux*. A ballet move," she added, and he guessed confusion had been on his face. "When two dancers stand on their toes and twirl about."

"I'll take your word for it." He arched his brows. "It'd be quite the sight to see those two big Highland cows dancing together." When she laughed, he waited, but she said nothing more as they reached the fence surrounding the field where the shaggy red cattle roamed. Instead she drew a single page out of the envelope. Its hot-pink hue made Abe chuckle.

"Dinah Shetler was a devout Amish woman," he said when he saw Jenna's puzzlement, "except she loved the brightest possible colors."

"She did. She used to tell me that while she kept the house within the parameters set forth by the church district, she'd also purchased vivid cooking utensils and stationery and yarn to make mittens and scarves for youngsters in the neighborhood. I don't think she ever got into trouble for it."

He reached across the fence and held out a single slice of apple. "As far as I know, she never drew the bishop's attention for her tiny rebellion. I do know local plain *kinder* were thrilled with her mittens, often with the image of a kitten or puppy knitted into the pattern. You liked them, too, ain't so?"

"I did, especially the year she made me hot-pink puppies

with bright blue spots. My friends loved them, so I let *Grossmammi* Dinah know."

"She made identical mittens for them, ain't so?" He kept his eyes on the two large cows lumbering toward him. The Highland cows made the Jerseys and Holsteins he milked look half-grown.

"Not identical. Theirs were blue puppies with pink spots."

"Dinah was always doing for others. Like every year when she made a pair of mittens and a matching scarf for you to take home to your sister. Susan must have been pleased with the gifts."

Jenna looked at the page. "Don't you think it's time to see what the second letter says?"

Knowing she was avoiding answering, he handed the rest of the apple to the cows. He wiped his hands. "Go ahead. Read it out loud."

He wasn't sure she'd agree, but she unfolded the page.

"My dearest Jenna,
"Did you figure out who should get the quilt? I'm sure you did, and I'm sure Sass taught you a lot about it. She'll enjoy learning if the quilt is as old as the note attached to it says.

Before I forget, I want you to give the Rickaboughs the three corn pails in the rear of the loafing shed."

"Loafing shed? What's that?" Jenna asked.

Abe pointed to the three-sided building where Dinah's buggy was parked. "Some folks call it an equipment shed, but it's also used for animals to get out of the sun or a storm. That's how it got its name. People saw the animals loafing around in the shade. What does the rest of the letter say?"

"Are you ready for your next puzzle? Let the geese fly south along the river to find their Joys. Let yourself join them, so you can find joys, too. On your way, make sure your cousins get a chance to kick the buckets down the road. They like to keep things extra quiet around their place, so it's time to make a racket and call some attention to them and what they're doing on their farm. Also giving them something may help keep them off your back for now."

"It's signed '*Grossmammi* Dinah.'" Jenna's frustration blared through her words. "I know I used to enjoy solving puzzles when I was a kid, but I'm not a kid any longer."

"No, you're not." He started to put a consoling hand on her shoulder, then thought better of it when he glanced at her dog. Buddy was silent, but watchful. The animal didn't need words to broadcast his distrust of Abe. His hackles were smooth, and his lips weren't pulled back. Still, Abe knew he'd be a fool to give the dog an excuse to believe he intended to hurt Jenna. "Dinah wanted those feed pails given to your cousin. I'll get them for you."

Abe appreciated the cooler shadows of the large lean-to. As he lifted the trio of galvanized pails, he noticed each had sizable dents in the sides. The quilt that Dinah had instructed to be given to Sass had been in nice shape. Why had the old woman decided to mention three banged-up pails?

As if he'd asked that aloud, Jenna gave him a quizzical expression as she followed him into the loafing shed. "Are you sure *those* are the ones she meant? They look like they're ready for the dump."

"The letter was specific. Three corn pails in the shed, ain't so?"

"These pails?" Her nose wrinkled, rearranging the scattering of freckles across her cheeks.

"Why are you hiding out here?" Daryl Rickabough peered into the shed.

"Daryl, how are you doing?" Jenna asked.

He ignored her question. "It's Tuesday. Letter day."

It was, but Abe didn't like how the other man held out his hand.

Jenna must not have either because she folded the letter and put it in the pocket of her shorts. Her tone was clipped. "There's no need for you to be concerned about this letter. It doesn't mention the farm."

"Nothing?"

"However, you're mentioned, Daryl." She took the buckets from Abe and held them out to her cousin. "Dinah asked me to give you these for your chickens."

"I don't need chicken feed buckets." He slapped one of the uprights supporting the slanted roof. "What did she think? That I was hand-feeding chickens?"

When Daryl didn't take the buckets, she set them on the ground. "All I know is what was in the letter. I don't think she's going to say anything about the farm and the house and the valuable pieces in there until the later letters."

He laughed. "Why do you think anyone would want Dinah's old junk? Did your brain get rattled in that explosion?"

Abe opened his mouth to warn her cousin to speak to her with respect, but she replied with a taut smile. "Sass Glick was delighted with the quilt *Grossmammi* Dinah left for her." She pointed at the buckets. "Just as she left these for you."

"They aren't worth much. Geneva isn't going to be overjoyed with this junk." In spite of his words, Daryl reached for the handles, hefted the buckets and walked away.

Jenna drew in a steadying breath. "Why does he have to make everything worse?"

Buddy rumbled something deep in his throat, and Jenna laughed.

"You're right, Buddy. He's a regular Mr. Sunshine."

Waiting until her cousin was out of earshot, Abe said, "Read the letter again. Out loud."

"Why?"

"Humor me. Daryl said something about Geneva being overjoyed. Wasn't there something about joy in the letter?"

She began to read it aloud.

He interrupted her when she spoke of flying geese. "Did you say Joyce?"

"It may be Joyce." Jenna tapped the page. "Joys has a capital letter for emphasis. Do you know a Joyce?"

"Joyce Allgyer is in the quilting group Dinah used to attend every week. Dinah must want her to have one of her quilts. *Komm mol.* I think I've got the answer you're looking for."

"Then what are we waiting for?"

Jenna didn't speak as she and Buddy followed Abe into the house. The dog went to his water bowl and lapped eagerly.

Going with Abe into the dining room, she stayed by the table as he walked past a quilting frame that sat empty beneath the double windows. He went to the shelves to the right of the windows. Sorting through the collection of quilts displayed along with clocks on one wall, he drew out a quilt and shook it open to reveal its pattern of colorful triangles against a white background. The triangles pointed in every possible direction.

"Where are the geese?" she asked.

"The triangles are supposed to be migrating geese. They fly in a vee." He set the quilt on the table and went to the hutch. Unlatching the glass door, he swung it aside and drew out a stack of small plates. "If you want my guess, the letter is referring either to that quilt or to these dishes."

Jenna couldn't keep from grimacing as she looked at the geese painted on the plates. Every feather was outlined, but she couldn't fail to notice the hunters who had their guns pointed at the bird in the center of the plate.

"These are hideous, Abe. Who would want to eat off a plate displaying the last moments of a bird's life?"

"Maybe Dinah was thinking of getting them out of the house so you didn't have to deal with them."

"No. The two letters have been specific on certain items going to someone who would appreciate them." She looked from the quilt to the dishes. "So which do you think she meant?"

"Take both. Maybe Dinah meant both. She was generous."

"I know." Again, she wondered, as she had before when she and Abe were talking about the mittens her grandmother had made, why Susan couldn't have—just once!—been grateful that *Grossmammi* Dinah had sent a gift home to her. Her half sister hadn't been related to Jenna's grandmother, but that hadn't stopped *Grossmammi* Dinah from considering her family.

"Susan is your sister," *Grossmammi* Dinah had said on multiple occasions. "You are my *kins-kind*. That makes us back door relatives."

When Jenna had asked what back door relatives were, her grandmother had explained they were people who didn't have to come to the front door like strangers. Jenna had been furious at the time, because her half sister had thrown away the cute mittens—they weren't stylish, Susan had asserted, and clashed with her winter coat.

Since her arrival in Sweetwater, Jenna had made only a quick call to let Mom know she and Buddy were safe. Though the call had lasted less than five minutes, somehow Mom had asked Jenna to get in touch with her sister.

"Susan's not sounding like herself," her mom had insisted.

Because Mom had been upset, Jenna had agreed to call her sister. And she did. Almost a half dozen times, leaving voice messages saying she hoped everything was okay with her sister.

Crickets.

That's what she'd gotten in return.

Squaring her shoulders and shrugging aside those uncomfortable thoughts, Jenna took the quilt and the ugly dishes from the dining room table. "Let's find out the answer to *Grossmammi* Dinah's puzzle."

Buddy didn't resist when Jenna told him to stay home while she went with Abe to take the quilt and dishes to a farm on the eastern side of Sweetwater. She guessed her partner didn't want to go out in the heavy humidity. Grateful for the air conditioning in her truck, she wasn't surprised when Abe took off his straw hat and fanned himself with it. She was grateful he'd agreed to come with her to the Allgyer house, because she knew the trip was delaying chores he wanted to get done. Though she considered asking him what he planned to do if *Grossmammi* Dinah hadn't left the farm to the Rickaboughs, she didn't. How could she ask him about his future plans when she didn't know her own? Not a single word had come from her supervisor in Philadelphia. She'd thought Vic Gould would have checked in at least once by now.

At a small ranch house set on a broad lawn, Abe told her to turn right. She drove past a sign stating "Allgyer Small Engine Repairs" and stopped in front of a garage that had been converted into a stable. Another building behind it must be where the shop was located.

Abe waited for her to collect the quilt and the dishes before he walked to the back door and opened it. "Anyone home?" he called.

Hearing footsteps, Jenna took a deep breath. She'd spent time with plain kids, but had always been uncomfortable with Amish adults other than her grandmother. It might have been because her mother, who was so glib, stumbled over her words around her late husband's family and neighbors. Mom had warned Jenna not to speak about her work.

"They consider it a sin to listen to the radio." Mom had always sounded incredulous. "Can you imagine how they must feel about a woman who makes her living on it? They believe a woman's place is in the kitchen. Nowhere else."

Jenna had argued, "*Grossmammi* Dinah never says anything bad about what you do."

"She never says *anything* about my job. It's like she thinks if she ignores it, I might stop doing the show that's the most important thing in the world to me."

Jenna had known better than to ask if her mother meant her radio show was the most important thing in the world to her after her family. Jenna had known, as her stepfather and Susan had, the number one thing in Marla in the Morning's life was the Marla in the Morning show.

"*Gute nammidaag,*" came a cheerful voice before a very tall woman in her early twenties appeared and pushed the door it open wider. The *kapp* on her light brown hair was even with the top of Abe's hat. Her blue gaze alighted on Jenna. "Good afternoon."

"Do you have a minute?" Abe asked.

"Certainly. I'm making cookies." She dimpled as her welcoming smile broadened. "I have samples."

He took a deep breath. "Smells like your cranberry chocolate chip cookies."

"With almonds."

Putting his hand over his heart, he said, "*Ach*, true happiness!"

The young woman laughed as Jenna followed Abe past a sparsely furnished living room and into a kitchen filled with many delicious aromas in addition to the cookies. By the sink, on the butcher block counter, a pair of cakes were cooling. One was chocolate cake with coconut frosting and the other one was an unfrosted cinnamon-spice cake, if Jenna's nose was right. For a moment, she wished she had Buddy's senses because she would have been able to identify even more of the distinct ingredients.

"Aren't you going to introduce us, Abe?" the woman asked.

"This is Jenna Shetler," Abe said as he stared at the rows of warm cookies on the table as if he were no older than the twins. He went on as he glanced at the woman who nodded before he selected a cookie for himself and another for Jenna, "I don't know if you remember her. Until about fifteen years ago, she used to come here to spend time with her *gross-mammi*. Dinah Shetler."

"You're Dinah's *kins-kind*?" The young woman's smile was for Jenna. "I'm sorry I didn't recognize you. We lived in a different district when you used to visit. I've heard you're handling Dinah's estate. Trust Dinah to make sure its dispersal is fun for everyone."

Jenna was taken aback. Why hadn't she imagined her grandmother had planned for the letters to be fun? *Gross-mammi* Dinah loved to bring smiles and happiness to everyone around her.

"So you're Joyce?" Jenna asked, feeling stupid, but Abe hadn't used the woman's name.

"*Ja*. Joyce Allgyer." She gave Abe a feigned frown. "Where are your manners, Abraham Bontranger?"

He mumbled something around a mouthful of cookie. Jenna was relieved his attention was on Joyce so he didn't see Jenna flinch. That last summer, when Jenna had been swallowed up by her teenage crush on him, she'd called him Abraham. Using it had seemed so grown-up, just like the feelings she had for him. Neither that infatuation nor her new name for him had lasted past the night when she'd told him about her feelings.

To hide her uncomfortable thoughts, she said, "Joyce, my grandmother wanted you to have this." She held out the quilt covered with the triangles.

"A flying geese quilt?" Puzzlement filled the brunette's

voice as she took the quilt from Jenna and opened it over a chair. "It's very nice, but I'm not sure why Dinah would want me to have this. It's not one of the quilts we worked on together. Dinah belonged to our small quilting circle. It's more accurate she was our teacher because she taught us so much about quilting. How to choose a pattern meaningful to us as well as how to pick colors."

"Bright ones, I assume."

Joyce grinned. "Always. There were times when we hid fabric so she wouldn't insist we include it in the quilt we were working on. We never did convince her fabric that would glow in the dark wasn't *gut* for a bed."

Laughing felt wonderful, and Jenna appreciated the other woman's attempts to put her at ease.

"What about the dishes, Jenna?" asked Abe, as he selected another cookie.

Jenna set them on the table.

"Oh, my!" Tears rushed into Joyce's eyes. "She remembered! These dishes used to belong to my *grossdawdi*. He adored them."

"Really?" The word slipped out before she could halt herself.

Joyce smiled through tears. "He said it reminded him of when he and your *grossdawdi* used to hunt along the river. They brought home more fish than fowl. To be honest, I've always believed they preferred to fish, but then my *grossdawdi* found these plates. My *grossmammi* didn't like them and gave them to Dinah after *Grossdawdi* died. I was heartbroken because I didn't want to lose them, because they connected me to him."

Her own eyes burned as Jenna realized her grandmother had seen the true value in the items she wanted to share. An antique quilt for a woman who loved to trace the history of quilts and now these plates that meant so much to a young woman.

"*Danki* for bringing them to me." Joyce held the topmost plate over her heart. "I'll treasure them as a gift from her as well as a memory of my *grossdawdi* and your kindness."

"As far as the quilt—"

"It was nice of you to bring it, but it would make me very happy if you found someone else who could use it." She brightened. "I know! I've heard you have a doggy partner. You should give it to him."

"A beautiful, handmade quilt like this?" She adored Buddy, but he'd be just as happy with a ragged old blanket as the quilt.

"*Ja.* A quilt is made with love, and Dinah loved you and your dog."

"She loved Buddy, too?" She looked at Abe who was regarding Joyce with surprise, too.

"She spoke often of how glad she was that you had your dog with you in the big city. Dinah would have been pleased for him to use one of her quilts."

Somehow, Jenna kept her sobs hidden inside her as she took the quilt and left the Allgyers' house, after accepting Joyce's invitation to visit the quilting group during her stay to meet her grandmother's other friends. She didn't let the tears loose while she took Abe back to the farm. She left him to do chores and called to Buddy to join her in the truck. Abe tried to get her to wait, but she didn't listen. She had to get away.

Now!

She drove a few miles before pulling over. Leaning her arms on the steering wheel, she propped her head on them and wept. Just hearing *Grossmammi* Dinah had been grateful for Buddy brought forth grief she hadn't realized was lurking in her heart. She cried for the woman who'd always been in her corner.

Buddy's cool nose poking at her face urged her to raise her

head sometime later. She wasn't sure how much later, because she hadn't paid attention to the time when she drove away from the farm, desperate to be alone. It was now after four, though it was as dark as midnight as storm clouds swarmed overhead.

What a day! Would the next four Tuesdays be like this? Filled with surprises and emotions she couldn't control?

"Just stay with me, Buddy." She buried her face in his fur.

He nuzzled her again, and she laughed when he stuck his nose in her ear. It was his signal for her to get over herself. He'd used it often when she'd been fighting depression after the explosion.

"Thank God for you," she murmured. Buddy was a gift from God, a partner who never asked more of her than he gave himself.

A soft cry came from deep in his throat as lightning flicked in the distance. She started the truck, hoping the sound of the engine would drown out any thunder. Overhead, thunderheads thickened, and she knew she should get inside before the storm reached them. Loud thunderclaps were one of Buddy's triggers.

"Let's go." She turned the truck onto the narrow road. Buddy licked her face, then his whimpers filled the truck as another bolt seared the sky. She pushed harder on the pedal.

Rain fell. Hard, in a silvery curtain her headlights couldn't pierce more than a few feet.

She swept out her arm to hold Buddy back as she slammed on the brakes. Something was in the road right ahead of them.

Pulling to the side, she activated her four-ways and opened the door. Buddy jumped down before she could halt him. She was about to call him when he raced to the dark item and gave a heartbreaking cry from deep in his throat. A sound she'd heard once before. When he was in her arms as debris fell around them and the explosion resonated in her aching ears.

She followed Buddy. There, in the middle of the lane, was

a puppy. It clambered to its feet and swayed. Its black-and-white face seemed to have no fur. As she took a step forward, she saw its fur was so filthy and matted it clung like a mask to the sides of the puppy's jaw.

"What are you doing out here on your own?" she asked, holding her hand so the pup could sniff it.

The tiny creature's rear dropped to the road. As Buddy inched forward, the puppy stared at him and stood. It began to cry out in obvious pain. Buddy bumped the puppy with his nose. Gently, but it was enough to knock the unsteady animal off its feet again. It curled into a ball and shivered.

When Buddy looked at her, he didn't need words to communicate that he wanted her help with the little puppy. Jenna didn't hesitate. Lifting the puppy, she wrinkled her nose when she smelled the hideous odor coming from its fur. Had it been sleeping in its own filth?

Now, as the rain pelted them, wasn't the time to figure out what had happened. It was the time to get them home and out of the storm. Once Buddy felt he was safe from the lightning and thunder and the puppy was clean and dry, then she could find out why a little puppy—it couldn't be more than a month old—was in the middle of the road on its own.

Chapter Six

It was the worst time for her phone to be dead. Jenna tried to turn it on and got nothing. She threw her truck in gear and raced toward the farm. She needed to find a veterinary clinic. The puppy was emaciated, and its feet looked like they'd been lacerated. Its breathing was labored.

Beside her, his nose against the silent puppy which she'd put in a cardboard box to keep it safe, Buddy acted as if the day was calm and sunny, so focused on the pitiful puppy he could ignore the thunderstorm. The sky was alight with so much lightning, she couldn't tell when one bolt had extinguished itself and another began.

She pulled into the drive and stopped. Buddy made soft noises. Knowing the puppy needed more than loving yips, Jenna reached for the door handle. She was as close to the house as she could get, but there was still more than fifteen feet between her and the porch steps.

"God," she whispered as she put one of *Grossmammi* Dinah's quilts under and over the puppy, "be with us and keep the storm from striking us. Keep this little one alive until we can get to the vet." Looking at Buddy, she asked, "Are you ready?"

He put his chin on her lap, and she ruffled his hair, grateful for his loyalty and devotion.

The puppy whimpered.

The sound galvanized her. Jenna opened the truck doors,

letting Buddy out while she lifted the tiny puppy. Her partner was steady against the strong wind and paid no attention to the rain. His gaze was focused on what Jenna carried.

Hurrying toward the house, having to pause once and then a second time as the wind tried to push her back, she struggled to protect the puppy from the rain. It seemed impossible when the wind lashed the trees, trying to turn them inside out. Lightning was a constant glow, and the thunder didn't rumble. It cracked like a giant whip. The rain blinded her, so she depended on Buddy to lead the way.

Then the rain stopped. No, it hadn't stopped, but it wasn't falling on her.

She raised her head and saw a large umbrella. Abe held it, and he put his arm around her waist to keep her on her feet. When she asked where he'd come from, he shook his head. She understood. It wasn't time for questions. Together they stumbled toward the house where Buddy was climbing the steps.

By the time she'd done the same and rushed through the screened porch to enter the house, she felt as battered as if she'd just finished a training session or a physical therapy appointment.

"Are you okay?" Abe asked.

"I am, but you're soaked." She cradled the puppy as she stared at him. When he removed his hat, his hair was plastered to his skull. His clothes hung on him with the weight of the rain. Water pooled under his work boots, and more dripped onto the floor as he lowered the umbrella and closed it.

"You look like a drowned kitten yourself."

"When my hair dries, I'll look like a very angry kitten. Thanks for helping us inside." Not giving him a chance to answer, she continued, "Do you know if regular milk is okay for puppies?"

His brows rose. "What?"

She cradled the puppy's box against her as she pointed at

it. "I found a puppy on the road, and I want to feed it, but I don't know if it should have cow's milk."

"How old is it?"

"I don't know. I've never raised a puppy. Buddy was full-grown when we were partnered."

Abe moved so close she was aware of every inch of him. Out in the yard, he'd put his arm around her, but then she'd been thinking of getting the dogs in out of the rain. Now, when he stood only the breadth of her fingers away, every breath she took was in unison with his. Did their hearts beat at the same tempo? Did his pulse leap when he bent toward her, or was he focused on what she held?

Buddy pushed between them.

Startled as her connection with Abe shattered, she said, "Buddy, it's okay. Just Abe. It's okay, Buddy. Abe wants to help. Just Abe."

Her partner gazed at her, his eyes flicking toward the puppy, but as she repeated, "Just Abe," he gave a single wag of his tail. It was his sign of reluctant obedience. Buddy didn't want Abe near the puppy, but he'd obey her.

"It's okay, Abe." She realized she'd used the same words as with the dog.

A swift smile warmed Abe's eyes behind his water-spotted glasses before he nodded. She was surprised when he spoke to her dog. "Buddy, I must check your tiny friend. Let me help Jenna take care of him."

Not sure how much Buddy comprehended, Jenna was relieved when the German shepherd dropped to the floor and rested his snout on his front paws. His eyes were trained on the three of them.

She held the box so Abe could get a better look. His breath was a sharp intake. "It can't be more than three or four weeks old. At this age, it's nursing. Without its *mamm*, it's going to depend on you for food."

"That's why I asked you if cow's milk is okay for a puppy."

He shook his head as she placed the box on the table. "It needs to have puppy milk replacer. It's like *boppli* formula. For now, you can give it some of Buddy's dry food with a lot of sterile water in it. Make it super soft." He put two fingers out to its tiny head. "It looks like a border collie. The black-and-white fur and the white end of its tail."

She plugged in her phone, then realized Abe should be able to answer her question. "Do you know a good vet around here?"

"*Ja*. Louis and Blondie Keel have a clinic on the other side of the river." He reeled off the address, pausing as lightning flashed like a Klieg light through the house. "Louis takes care of the animals here. Blondie focuses on smaller animals."

They froze when thunder erupted. Buddy let out a howl. Her eyes were caught by Abe's, and she saw the same trepidation in them that whirled through her heart. Was Buddy's reaction because the puppy had died? Or had it been just the clap of thunder?

Jenna peered into the box. The puppy's sides were moving. She glanced at the window where rain pelted the glass. No flashes crisscrossed the clouds, so she picked up the box. A clatter halted her.

She looked into the box. She'd been sure the box was empty before she put the quilt and puppy in it. "Oh, my!"

"What is it?" Abe's concern laced through his question.

"On our way here, Buddy must have put his favorite toy in the box for the puppy." Tears flooded her eyes, shocking her. She'd thought she'd cried out all she had earlier. "Good boy, Bud."

The dog's tail wagged, his eyes focused on the box. She didn't bother trying to convince him to stay at the house while she took the puppy to the vet.

Abe offered to hold the umbrella over the box. When she was

about to climb into the truck, he said, "Jenna, I need to get back to the barn. One of the cows isn't doing well, and I need to—"

"Take care of the cow. That's what *Grossmammi* Dinah would have wanted you to do. We'll be fine."

"All right. Watch out for water in low areas of the road. I'll be praying for all of you."

"I never doubted that." For Abe, his faith was like the umbrella, protecting and dependable and unpretentious. She envied him the certainty his prayers would be heard and answered. He believed in a devoted Father. Maybe because he had one. She never had, and her relationship with God was more hit-and-miss. She didn't doubt His love. She simply didn't believe He listened.

As she headed toward the clinic, she had to hope Abe's prayers would be heard and answered.

It took longer than Abe had expected for Jenna to return from the veterinary clinic. He'd finished work in the barn just as the rain eased to a drizzle, then stopped. When the twins had appeared, soaked to the skin, he wasn't surprised to hear that they'd taken a "shortcut" through the woods between their house and Dinah's farm after Sara Beth sent them over so she could go to work. Now they were playing checkers on the screened porch, waiting for Jenna to arrive back with the puppy they were eager to meet. They'd asked questions he couldn't answer about what type of dog it was and what it'd been doing in the road.

He'd pondered those questions himself while he finished tending the cow in the barn. For more than an hour, he'd sat, rocking and watching while he watched the animals in the fields. The Highland cows had tried to convince him to give them more treats, but he'd ignored them and they'd gone to the hayrack in the middle of the field. As the sun began to set in the sodden aftermath of the storm, he'd checked on the other animals, making sure the chickens were in their coop for the.

The truck's lights were the first signal Jenna was slowing to turn into the drive. She drove as if she carried stacks of fine china.

A *gut* sign, he told himself, because that meant the puppy was in the truck.

When she stopped the truck and got out, he stood, but didn't go down the steps. He didn't want to get in the way and risk hurting the puppy by causing Jenna to slip in the mud. As well, he wasn't sure how Buddy would react to him.

"Puppy!" cried Zoe as she jumped to her feet. The checkers and the board went flying in every direction. She and Zeke grumbled at the momentary delay in greeting the puppy as they began to gather them up, giving Jenna a chance to walk past them.

God, danki *for Your perfect timing*. Abe didn't smile as he stepped aside, holding the door as Jenna carried the blanket-draped box into the house.

When Buddy pushed past him, Abe watched the dog, which considered the puppy his. Abe entered the kitchen as Jenna put the box on the floor.

"Dr. Blondie said not to put the box on the table." She squatted with care, balancing herself with her hand on a chair. "If the pup climbs out, it would easy to tumble off the table. Here on the floor is better."

"Are you okay doing that?" he asked before he could halt himself. Fool! Hadn't he learned Jenna didn't like to show any weakness?

"I'm okay doing this. I'm not supposed to kneel. I may need help getting up. Getting older, you know."

He smiled at her attempt at humor. "*Ja*. Thirty is ancient." A motion in the box caught his eye. "How's the pup?"

"In pretty bad condition."

He sighed. "I'm sorry to hear that. Zoe and Zeke have been diligent in praying it'll survive."

"Dr. Blondie said the next twelve hours will be the most crucial. We just have to hope the puppy's still alive in the morning. If—"

The front door opened and slammed. Buddy jumped to his feet, his hackles raised. He calmed when the twins ran in.

Abe held them away from the box. "You need to be quiet. We've got one very sick puppy here."

Jenna snorted what might have been a muffled laugh. He wasn't sure what was amusing.

"Can I pet him?" Zoe asked the moment Abe released her.

"Not now," Jenna answered at the same time he did; then she added, "The puppy needs to sleep right now, and the puppy is a she."

"It— She looks ugly." Zeke tried to edge past Abe to get a better look.

Grasping his brother by his suspenders, Abe said, "You've seen the puppy. Now go and enjoy the tire swing."

The twins began to protest, but he cut them off with a glance toward the front door. "The puppy needs to sleep so she can grow big and strong."

"Is she sick?" Zoe's eyes filled with tears. "Is God going to call her home?"

"*Ja*, she's very sick."

"I'm going to pray she's okay soon."

"Me, too!" Zeke added before grabbing his sister's hand. "*Komm mol*. Let's finish our game."

Zoe hesitated. "The puppy needs a name."

"Jenna rescued the puppy," Abe said, "so she should name her."

"We've been praying hard for her," Zeke argued. "Doesn't that mean *we* should name her?"

Jenna smiled. "Have you two picked out a name?"

"Pal," the twins said as one.

"Pal?" Abe repeated, surprised at the simple name. He'd expected them to pick something outrageous. They'd had a kitten named Princess Monkey Toes.

"*Ja*." The tilt of Zoe's chin reminded him too much of his own. "It's a *gut* name, and I like it and Zeke likes it. What do you think, Jenna?"

"I think none of us is the expert." She put her hand on Buddy's head. "What do you think? Is Pal a good name for the pup?"

Buddy gave a short bark that sounded like an assent.

"Everyone agrees." Jenna levered herself to stand. "Now Pal needs to rest."

Zeke turned to go, but Zoe didn't move. "You've got a make-believe leg. Why doesn't Buddy have a make-believe leg?"

Jenna smiled. "Buddy wasn't a candidate for a prosthesis because of the way his leg was amputated."

"Pal will love him anyhow." Zoe blew a kiss to the dog. "Just as I do."

Abe shooed them toward the door and closed it behind them. Kneeling by the box, he bowed his head and sent up a prayer for healing. And for them to accept God's will if the puppy didn't survive.

Jenna watched him with a pensive expression. "It must have been a shock when the twins were born."

"I had several months to prepare." He stood, taking care he didn't step on Buddy.

"Flossie, who had been the youngest, must have been in school when the twins arrived."

"*Ja*, Flossie was in first grade when Zeke and Zoe were born. It was a big change to have *bopplin* in the house again."

She lit the stove under the kettle, and he hoped she was heating water for *kaffi*. "I know your family. Those babies were handed off to you."

"When they were little, it wasn't hard. It was when they learned to walk and to talk—and to talk back—that my life became complicated again."

Going to the cupboard, she got two cups. She put instant *kaffi* on the counter along with the tea canister. When she motioned for him to choose which he wanted, he opened the *kaffi* container. She held out a spoon, which he took.

"Abe, can I ask you something?"

"Go ahead."

"What happened when your right hand was bitten?"

"I trusted the wrong dog." He explained how the attack had been abrupt and without any warning. The only thing he could guess that had provoked the dog was he'd grabbed Zeke away before the dog could clamp its teeth on his brother's tiny arm. "Zeke wasn't hurt," he finished. "I thank God every day for that."

She took his hand and tilted it over on her palm. When she ran her fingers along his, he could barely hear her over the hammering of his heart. "I'm sorry Buddy came roaring at you the day I arrived."

"It was unnerving." *Almost as unnerving as your touch is right now.* He drew away his hand before he could give into his yearning to tell her how often he'd thought of her—every day and every night since her arrival. "Buddy doesn't seem to want to share you."

"He wants to protect me. Richard couldn't understand that."

"Richard?"

"My ex. He made himself scarce after I got home from rehab, but things hadn't been going well for quite a while."

"Why?"

He could see she wished that she'd never brought up the topic. There was a long silence before she said, "He was jealous of the time I spent with work and with Buddy. He thought my world should revolve around him."

Talking about her failure with her former fiancé was pain-ful, he could tell. She didn't like to fail at anything.

"I'm sorry," he said, as she had a moment ago.

Jenna didn't answer as Buddy whined. Going to the box, she comforted her partner. "You're going to have to be patient, Buddy. We've got to give Pal time to heal."

"Heal?" Abe asked as he lifted the kettle off the stove and filled his cup and hers, making sure the string on her teabag didn't slip into the hot water. "Was the puppy injured on the road?"

"No." Her hand seized the edge of the table, and he saw her muscles strain with her attempt to control her outrage. "The puppy was injured before. The wounds and broken bone in her tail have partially healed, so the vet thought the damage was done almost a week ago." Her voice broke. "Who would do such a thing to a little puppy?"

He shook his head. "I wish I could tell you, Jenna, but you heard about the puppy mills rumored to be around here."

"Dr. Blondie said Pal may have escaped from one. The lacerations on her paws are the tip-off that she'd been kept in a wire cage with no protection for her feet. The blood on her fur wasn't all hers, so the rest of her litter must be suffering." Her jaw worked before she spit out, "If I ever find who's mis-treating dogs like this, you're going to have to hold me back before I do something I *won't* regret."

"I can't promise that."

"Because plain folks don't make promises?"

"Because I'd be as furious as you are."

Her rage sifted away. Knowing her as he did, he realized she'd never step outside the law to invoke vengeance on the cruel people who cared more about money than living crea-tures.

"You're a good man, Abe Bontranger." She put her hand on his arm.

He slid his hand over hers, not wanting to let her slip away. Her skin felt so *wunderbaar*, soft and yet strong at the same time. Wasn't that the definition of Jenna Rose Shetler? A mercurial wisp, flitting here and there, while at the same time she was one of the most grounded, sensible people he'd ever met.

And the most beautiful. It was true her pale hair was frizzed out to twice its normal size, and her eyes were red-rimmed from tears she'd shed. Her eyes were usually the color of hydrangea blossoms, the perfect complement to her deep pink lips. A man could lose himself in dreaming of tasting her mouth.

When she pulled away, Abe had no idea how much time had passed. Long enough for her tea to steep. She took out the bag and reached for the fridge door to get *millich*.

That allowed him time to rope his thoughts into his control. "The *gut* Lord implored Adam and his descendants to tend to this earth and the creatures on it."

"Is that why you make an extra effort to tend to Dinah's animals?" The faintest quiver told him she wasn't as unmoved by his touch as she pretended. "The Highland cows come running when you're near the fence. They don't do that for anyone else. I don't think it's just because you bring them treats. I think it's because they know you care about them."

He wished she wasn't so insightful. It must have been a great asset for her as a police officer, but he didn't appreciate how she saw past his facade. She might find the man he didn't want anyone to see. The man who struggled to be the *gut* son and the faithful man everyone believed him to be. The man who always said, "*Ja*," when someone needed help, while at the same time being the man who had cruelly tossed aside Jenna's love one summer years ago.

A man who had lost his way after that night and had no idea how to find it again.

Chapter Seven

Gunfire!

Jenna would have recognized that sound anywhere. Who was shooting in Sweetwater after dark? What was going on?

The gun sounded again, and Buddy rushed to her.

She was ready to jump out of bed, then remembered she had a single leg. It had taken only one time of falling on her face to teach her caution.

A fist pounded on the door downstairs. Shocked, she pulled her robe over her pajamas, then turned on her flashlight and flung open the window beside the bed. "Who's there?"

"Sara Beth. Sara Beth Bontranger."

Abe's sister? What was the teen doing here at—Jenna squinted at the bedside clock—at two fifteen in the morning? With someone firing a gun?

"Come inside! Now!" she called, fearing a stray bullet would find Sara Beth.

Buddy gave her a concerned glance.

"It's okay, Buddy. Same old, same old." Though it wasn't. Who was shooting a gun in the middle of the night in Sweetwater?

As the German shepherd went to the box where the puppy was sleeping, Jenna called to Sara Beth that she'd be down in a minute. It didn't take much longer than that now for her to settle her prosthesis around what remained of her leg. She could have used the crutches she kept by her bed, but some remnant of vanity or pride insisted she stand on her own.

She went down the dusky stairs. Sara Beth waited in the hall. In the glow from Jenna's flashlight, she could see the teen was dressed in a light green dress with a black apron over it, but she had boots on her feet that had left wet footprints across the porch. Her black hair was hidden beneath a white kerchief. A small battery-powered lantern was in her hand.

"What are you doing here?" Jenna asked.

"I was on my way home, and I heard shooting. Your house was closest."

"Does Abe know you're out at this hour?"

Sara Beth shook her head, her teeth chattering. Not with cold, because the night was almost as hot and sticky as the day had been. Was it fear?

"Do you know who's shooting, Sara Beth?" Jenna asked.

"N-n-no." A hiccuped sob burst out of her.

Jenna's temper flared so fast she couldn't halt it. Her voice rose on every word. "Have you lost every bit of sense you've ever had? Why are you running around at night? You should have hunkered down behind a tree or a bush where you were. Someone firing a rifle after dark can't see what's beyond his target."

"It's a rifle?" Sara Beth shuddered from head to her boots. "I wasn't sure."

"I'm not one hundred percent sure either," she admitted as she raised the window she'd closed earlier so the rain wouldn't drip in. Holding up her hand, she held her breath as another report echoed through the night. Whoever was shooting was farther along the road. "Stay here."

"You aren't going out there!"

"Stay *here*!" She pointed at the dining room wall, which was away from the windows and the door. As soon as the girl moved to what Jenna hoped was a safe spot, she headed back upstairs to her room. Walking around Buddy, who was as close to Pal's box as he could get, she opened the top drawer of the oak dresser. Pulling out her weapon, she slapped in the magazine. She ordered Buddy to stay with Pal as she walked out. She didn't want him running outside and being hit. She didn't release the safety on her handgun as she went downstairs. Not lighting any of the propane lights on the first floor, she edged past Sara Beth and out the front door.

She halted on the porch and gave her eyes time to adjust to the darkness. As stars became visible among the thick clouds, she peered through the trees toward the river. The shots had sounded closer than that.

After five minutes of silence, she guessed whoever had been shooting had stopped. She released the magazine and balanced it in her hand as she went into the house. Sara Beth met her at the door.

"Nothing." Jenna put the empty gun and the magazine on the dining room table. "No more shooting. Is there any open hunting season now?"

"Coyotes and foxes and woodchucks can be hunted all year." Sara Beth held her arms close to her body.

"That makes sense. Someone may have seen a fox or a coyote near one of their chicken houses." She smiled. "I don't think anyone is trying to get rid of a groundhog in the middle of the night by shooting into its burrow."

Abe's sister didn't smile as she'd hoped. In fact, the girl looked ready to cry.

"Sara Beth, what's wrong? Why are you out at this time of night?"

"I couldn't sleep so I thought I'd go for a walk."

"Why couldn't you sleep?"

The girl didn't hesitate. As if she'd been waiting for that question, the words burst past her lips. "I might be pregnant."

Putting her arm around Abe's sister's shoulders, Jenna

steered her into the living room. She sat Sara Beth in a comfortable chair, then lit the propane lamp hanging from the ceiling. Taking a seat in the middle of the couch, she clasped her hands on her lap.

"Why are you telling me this?" Jenna asked.

"Abe says you've always been *gut* with keeping secrets."

She sighed. Not telling anyone she and Abe, when they were twelve, had "borrowed" a pair of kayaks and paddled down the Pocomoke River almost to its mouth was very different from not revealing to Abe's parents that their oldest daughter might be pregnant.

"So Abe knows?"

"He's the only one. Other than you." She hung her head. "I shouldn't have told you, but I needed to tell another woman."

Another woman? Sara Beth couldn't be more than sixteen. That was a girl in Jenna's estimation.

Instead she listened as Sara Beth added, "I asked Abe not to say anything to *Mamm* and *Daed* until I was sure."

"You aren't sure? What did the doctor say?"

Color rose up her cheeks. "I haven't seen a *doktor* yet."

"Why not?"

"I want to give it enough time. One of my friends thought she was going to have a *boppli*. When she found out she wasn't pregnant, her boyfriend broke up with her and married someone else. I don't want to lose Kenny."

Trying to get her mind around teenage logic, Jenna asked, "Is he your boyfriend?"

"*Ja.*"

"What did he say when you told him?"

Sara Beth squirmed on the chair. "I haven't told him. Not yet. I don't want to upset him."

"So you weren't joking when you said the only person you've told is Abe."

"*Ja*." Her gaze focused on her thumbs on the top of her other fingers.

"Sara Beth—"

"Don't tell me I'm stupid. I know that."

Jenna stretched forward to put her hand over the younger woman's and gave a silent sigh when she felt how hard Sara Beth was trembling. "I wasn't going to say you were stupid. I've called myself that enough times already."

"Because you weren't able to get out of the way of an explosion?"

She winced as the teenager poked the rawest spot in her heart. Was it so obvious to everyone? Knowing if she wanted Sara Beth to be honest, she must be as forthright, Jenna said, "Because I couldn't get Buddy and myself out of the way."

As if she'd shouted her partner's name, Buddy came padding in with his uneven gait. He looked in her direction, then went to sit beside Sara Beth. He leaned against her, offering her silent consolation.

"Nobody can move fast enough to get out of the way of an explosion." Sara Beth slipped off her chair, knelt and fluffed the fur around Buddy's ears.

The dog closed his eyes in delight, then licked Sara Beth's wet cheek. When she flung her arms around him, Buddy looked at Jenna. At that moment, Jenna was sure the dog would have shrugged his shoulders if he'd been able to.

Reaching out, Jenna stroked the younger woman's head. "You need to see a doctor, Sara Beth. It's important for your health and for your baby's. I'll go to the doctor with you unless you have a friend you want to go with you."

"I do. You."

"Why me?"

"I remember you from when I was little. You didn't call me a boring *boppli* as Abe's other friends did."

Jenna smiled. "They called me the same thing."

"They called *you* that? You're a police officer, and you've got a bomb-sniffing dog as a partner. How could anyone call you boring?"

"I wasn't an officer when I was a kid. I was just a tagalong pest."

"Who called you that?"

"Your brother. A bunch of times."

Sara Beth shook her head in disgust. "Boys are slow to get their brains functioning. I've heard *Mamm* say that when my brothers interrupted her at work, and she struggled to hold on to her patience." She pushed herself to her feet. "I should go. If he discovers I'm out so late, Abe will be worried."

Abe would be worried. It seemed that was another thing that hadn't changed. Ezekiel and Barbara put their attention on their business, leaving Abe to raise his siblings. Though she knew it was an accepted expectation that older children raise the younger ones, Abe was more of a parent to the other Bontrangers than their own mother and father.

Maybe that's why she and Abe had gotten on so well. Neither of them had ever had parents they could depend on because their parents thought of their work more than their kids. She tried to recall if she and Abe had ever spoken of such things. Probably not. As youngsters, they'd accepted their lives as they were.

When she walked with Jenna to the front door, Sara Beth paused. "You know he doesn't think that any longer, ain't so?"

"He? Abe?"

"*Ja*, he doesn't believe you're a tagalong pest now. In fact, if you want my opinion, he's the tagalong now, not you. He uses any excuse to *komm* over here." Her smile became sly. "So do you think he's a pest or not?"

Not wanting to answer the unanswerable, Jenna mumbled something that she hoped sounded like "be careful" and "hurry home," before she shut the door. It wasn't so easy to ignore the question, however. It kept her awake until dawn.

Jenna stopped at her cousins' farm the next day on her way back from doing errands in Sweetwater. Their conversation was short and to the point because they didn't invite Jenna into the house. They hadn't heard any gunshots the previous night.

"We're heavy sleepers," Geneva said.

How could she argue with that? It was difficult to believe the Rickaboughs hadn't heard anything last night. The shooting had sounded as if it was close to their farm. Short of calling Geneva—and Daryl who nodded to confirm his wife's comment—liars, there wasn't anything she could do.

"Can you get Ken to give you the rest of the letters now? He's got to know how eager we are." Daryl eyed her up and down. "Especially Abe."

She wanted to tell him not to use Abe's yearning to have his own farm as a way to manipulate her. "This is how *Grossmammi* Dinah wanted it, and Ken won't go against her request." It took more willpower than she'd expected to force a smile, and she wasn't surprised when Buddy bumped her gently. With his ability to gauge her emotions, he must be able to tell she was annoyed with her cousins' greedy and disrespectful questions. However, she kept her voice unagitated with the skills she'd learned for defusing tense situations. "I need to get home. See you later."

"You will," Daryl called after her, making it sound like a threat.

Jenna dragged her frustration home. It deepened when she realized she'd missed Abe doing the chores. She wanted to talk to him about his sister's visit last night, but he was nowhere to be found.

A quick check told her that Pal was sound asleep. Dr. Blondie had warned the antibiotics she'd prescribed often caused drowsiness. Jenna paused by the box and resisted the longing to reach out and pet the little creature, whose tail was wrapped in gauze. Clasping her hands behind her, she contented herself by watching the black-and-white puppy's slow, steady breathing.

Her sense of futility returned, and she knew the way to deal with it was to find something to do. She considered going to the attic and finding the old, tattered quilts to give to Sass, but it would be like a broiler under the eaves. That would have to wait for a cooler day.

She carried the puppy's box downstairs and onto the screened porch. Pal didn't stir.

Pouring herself some lemonade, she glanced around the empty fridge. Grocery shopping needed to be on her to-do list if she was going to have food tomorrow. She missed the ease with which she could call a restaurant and have food delivered within minutes.

Buddy followed and dropped to the boards next to the box. Looking at her, he raised his light brown eyebrows and gave her a doggy grin.

"You could use a grooming." She'd been running him through the fields, following the scents she'd prepared. It was part of his training to become a search-and-rescue dog.

Though she'd been kept busy doing as *Grossmammi* Dinah's letters had requested, she yearned for the excitement of the job she'd left behind in Philadelphia. Her sole call to the precinct had been unsatisfactory. Everyone had been busy with cases she wasn't familiar with, and the phone at that end had been passed from desk to desk with nobody talking to her for more than a couple of minutes. Their lives had gone on without her.

Her dog wagged his tail, thumping it on the porch as she went in to get his brush. When she sat facing him again, she drew the stiff bristles along his spine before focusing on his ruff.

Buddy gave a soft sound deep in his throat, and she smiled.

Her beloved dog loved these grooming times as much as she did. It reinforced the connection between them. Most K-9 handlers agreed such bonding time was as important as training hours.

He stiffened. When Jenna saw Abe approaching, she didn't stop brushing, murmuring to Buddy to relax. However, her eyes were on Abe's easy motions as he crossed the yard. There was something so light about him, yet so grounded at the same time.

Abe climbed the steps and opened the door to the porch. "Am I intruding?"

She almost said yes. For years, she hadn't thought about Abe Bontranger. Now he seemed constantly to be in her head.

Don't be silly, she told herself. *Of course, he's in your thoughts. He's helping you with* Grossmammi *Dinah's will, and he's taking care of the animals here on the farm. Why wouldn't you be thinking of him?*

"Come in," she replied.

Buddy rose, shook his coat from his nose to the tip of his tail and edged away far enough to give Abe room to sit.

"How's Pal doing?" Abe sat in the other rocker.

"Sleeping. She's doing a lot of sleeping."

"Best medicine."

She smiled. "I thought laughter was supposed to be the best medicine."

"Dogs don't laugh."

"You haven't been around when Buddy saw me tumble over while he pranced around me." Putting the brush on the table beside her, she asked, "Do you want lemonade?"

"*Danki*, but not right now. If I want a glass, I know where to get one."

"True." She knew he'd been in and out of the house for as long as she had. "Have you been working at your parents' shop?"

He looked at his trousers and brushed away sawdust. "I have, but this is from work on a project that's not a shed."

"What is it?"

"A boat."

Her brows rose. "You've got a boat?"

"Why are you surprised? I've been talking about wanting one for years."

"Not to me."

He paused, then nodded. "Now that I think about it, I didn't begin talking about a boat until after you stopped coming here. For the past few years, I've been rehabbing an old wooden boat."

"Inboard or outboard? My stepfather has an inboard one."

"I thought your family lives in Las Vegas. Isn't that in the desert?"

"It is, but Lake Mead isn't far away."

"It can't be like boating in Chesapeake Bay. Have you ever been on the bay?"

"No."

"Never?" He looked at her as if she'd admitted she walked only on her hands. "You need to take time to do that while you're here. If nothing else, take a ferry to one of the islands."

"Let's see if I have time. This week's letter was quick to figure out. Who knows how much time I'll need next week?"

Instead of answering, he leaned back and rocked. He watched as Pal shifted in her sleep, then stared at where Maeve and Maude were grazing. As the silence stretched between them, Jenna wondered how to tell him about his sister's visit in the middle of the night.

She decided there was no way other than saying it. As she started to do so, choosing her words with care, he stopped her.

"Sara Beth already told me how she came here last night when she heard someone firing a gun." His mouth twisted in a disgusted expression. "I don't know who was more stupid.

Her for going out, or the person shooting after dark. There are traps that can be set for predators." He glanced at her. "Sara Beth said you got your gun and went outside to make sure she and the dogs were safe."

"I did." She wasn't going to apologize for doing as she'd been trained to do.

"*Danki.*"

His simple gratitude pleased her. "The shooting was over by the time I came out. Abe, Sara Beth told me."

He blinked once, then a second time. "Did she? I didn't think she was going to talk to anyone about her situation."

Realizing he was being vague in case his sister had told her about something else, she said, "She needs to see a doctor. Sooner rather than later. So much can go wrong at the beginning of a pregnancy."

"I know, but she said she wanted to have time to be certain. I can't drag her to the *doktor*'s, ain't so?"

"She's a minor, so your parents could, but she hasn't told them." Jenna arched her brows. "She may be more cunning than I assumed. Teenagers have networks of information, even plain teens who aren't on social media."

He grimaced. "I wouldn't assume they're not on social media. Many of our teens have cell phones and other devices they keep hidden from adults."

"All the more reason to be concerned she knows more than she's letting on. You need to talk to her, Abe. I know the subject may not be comfortable—"

He halted the rocker. "She's my sister, Jenna. I'm not going to let discomfort get in the way of helping her."

"I'm glad to hear that."

"I'm glad to hear you understand teenagers so well." He put his hand on the arm of her chair, stopping it. "*Komm* with me to a youth group meeting and help me convince the teens they're slipping into dangerous territory."

"I told you I don't think it'll help. Get a local cop to come."

"No. I need *your* help!"

Abe wasn't surprised Jenna regarded him with her mouth half-open. He seldom was so vehement.

"I could use your help, Jenna. Elden told me about another break-in at a chicken farm east of Sweetwater. I can't put it off any longer."

"Do you and your bishop think if you gather the teens together and ask them about the mischief they'll be honest with you?"

"No."

"Good, because if you thought that you're doomed to failure. If you ask a local police officer—"

"Elden doesn't want to involve the authorities."

She stood and drained the last of her lemonade from her glass. He knew she was gathering her thoughts. "Abe, I doubt if anyone in Sweetwater hasn't learned by now that I'm a cop. Why would the kids talk to me?"

"Tell me something, Jenna."

"Anything."

He knew she thought she was being honest, so he didn't point out she kept a lot to herself. *You do, too*, warned that tiny voice he wished would stay quiet.

"Why did you become a cop? I knew you for years, and I never guessed you would decide to join the police. You weren't a—what do you call a person who never does anything wrong?"

"Impossible?"

He tried to douse his smile but couldn't. "No, I mean someone who always behaves him- or herself."

"A Goody Two-shoes?"

"That's the one."

Her eyes grew round. "Do you think cops start off as a Goody Two-shoes?"

"Don't they?"

"No. Plenty of us got into trouble when we were teens. That's when we first meet a police officer who cares about helping us more than seeing us punished for our mistakes. That's what happened to me. I'd been skating on the wrong side of the law for a while, and Officer Matt Boone inspired me to decide to stay on the straight and narrow as well as to eventually help others as he helped me. He served with the Washington State Patrol, and he reached out to me when our family lived in Seattle."

"I don't remember you living in Seattle."

"It was after I stopped spending summers here. I was in college when I met Matt. He pulled me over for speeding. That night I was furious, but somehow we started talking after I had to go to court. He saw something in me that I hadn't. With his help, I learned pushing limits so I could get someone to notice me wasn't the way to go. That's a lesson he wanted me to pass along to others, and I've tried."

Though Abe couldn't imagine how anyone could possibly overlook dynamic Jenna Rose Shetler, he guessed she was referring to her family. She never said a lot about them. Just enough for him to know she felt like an outsider in her own home with her ambitious *mamm* and her timid stepfather and her sister with whom she had nothing in common other than a *mamm* and an ever-changing address.

He came to his feet. "It sounds as if you became a cop to help people."

"That's one of the reasons I became a K-9 cop. People will stop and talk to you when you've got a dog, people who might be spooked by the uniform. When there was an opening in bomb detection, Buddy and I volunteered." She sighed. "I'm not saying that was the best decision I ever made."

"It was at the time." He put his fingers under her chin and

tipped it so their gazes met, then held. "How many bombs did you and Buddy find? How many lives did you save?"

"I didn't keep count. Nothing matters but being successful."

"So help me be successful, Jenna." His voice softened to a whisper. "Help me help these kids before they get in so much trouble they can't get out. Like Matt helped you."

She smiled, the expression creating lines at the corners of her eyes that he hadn't seen before. The warmth of her skin wafted toward his, and the luscious aroma of the lemonade she'd enjoyed lured him closer to her vibrant lips. Would they still have the sweet-sour flavor from the lemonade, or would they taste of her?

A low growl from the porch paralyzed every thought. Buddy pushed between him and Jenna. She bent to pet her dog, but Abe saw the warning in the German shepherd's eyes. Buddy might tolerate him as long as Abe didn't get too close to Jenna. Abe didn't want to mention the dog's reaction, because that might reveal how much he wanted to kiss her.

When she spoke, the moment had passed. He was filled with both relief and regret.

"There's one insurmountable problem, Abe. The kids will be speaking in *Deitsch*, and I don't know more than a few words. Those kids aren't going to be talking about *redding* up a room or drinking *kaffi* or *millich* with one's *schnitzboi*."

"Apple pie? You're making me hungry." He was glad his jest didn't fall flat. Not a jest, a lie. He could think of plenty beyond dessert, but each thought focused on how enticing her lips were.

"Be serious."

"I am. Listen, Jenna. Join me at the youth gathering and observe. You're sure to see things I won't. Or any other plain adult because we know these kids so well. You can focus on how they interact and what signals they give off. Maybe, just maybe, you'll discover something that will help us pinpoint the teens who need our assistance to stay out of trouble. Will you help?"

He held his breath as he waited for her decision. If she refused, he wasn't sure where he could turn next. He'd promised Elden, and just as important, he wanted to put an end to the pranks before someone was hurt.

It seemed to be an eternity before she responded. When it came, her answer was simple.

"Yes."

Chapter Eight

"Abe? You in here?" came his brother Benuel's voice.

"Abe! *Daed* wants to see you." That was Homer.

Both of his brothers stuck their heads around the door of the production shed, peered through the sawdust and then walked in. They were like identical peas in a pod, though they weren't twins. Less than a year had separated their births, and one was seldom seen without the other. Both were neatly dressed with their hair brushed, looking ready to pick up their favorite girl to take her home from a singing.

Except it wasn't Sunday evening. It was Tuesday morning. The day next letter from Dinah should be arriving.

Abe drew a plank out of the planer and set it on top of the rest in the pile by the side wall. A few more to do before he was finished with this batch, and then the team could cut the boards to size for his parents' bestselling sheds. A peaked roof, four walls with a window in each end and a set of double doors that opened in the center on one long side. With distributors waiting throughout the Northeast for the sheds, which had become popular in recent years after someone coined the terms "she shed" and "he shed," the team was working six days a week. The business needed more employees, but people with the skills required to build the sturdy sheds weren't easy to find, even when his parents offered bonuses to new hires who stayed for at least six months.

"*Daed* needed to send both of you here to get me?"

His brothers had the decency to look ashamed. Benuel elbowed Homer, and they walked away. Homer yawned, a sure sign his younger brother had been out late again last night. Abe hadn't heard the names of any possible women his brother might be walking out with, but it was clear Homer was growing more serious about her because he seldom came home before midnight.

Abe sighed as a feeling he didn't like ran through him. Envy. How he wished he could spend his time with a woman who'd caught his attention!

With Jenna.

He didn't try to silence that thought. It was the truth, and it was, he knew, one of the reasons he'd pushed her to help with the youth group. Trying to keep the kids out of trouble gave him the perfect excuse to spend time with her. That she could help the teens was important, but would he have pushed as hard for her help if he hadn't wanted to see her?

Sighing again, he went out the door. When his *daed* asked him to use the forklift to move a completed shed so it could be loaded on a flatbed later, Abe pushed thoughts of Jenna from his mind. It took every ounce of his attention to make sure the shed was secure and didn't tumble off the forks. He was grateful for the respite from his own thoughts...at least for a short while.

Abe heard a shout from the old garage behind Dinah's house as he came out of the barn later that morning to dump buckets of water that he'd used to wash the floor. Who was in there? The roof had more holes than shingles, and the walls tilted at an alarming angle. If someone was in there, they could get hurt.

Dropping the buckets, he ran to the garage. He couldn't see through the shadows. "Who's there? Are you okay?"

A silhouette moved and became solid. "Abe, it's Jenna, and I'm fine." She pulled out a tissue and dabbed at her bloody knee. He remembered her having plenty of scrapes when she'd been a kid in Sweetwater.

He edged around a rusting car that was older than his *daed*. Auto parts and dirt-crusted metal made the garage's interior a slalom course. Digging his bandana from his pocket, he knelt and wrapped it around her knee. He tied it off and stood. Had she felt how his fingers quivered while his cheek was so close to her skin?

"You should go into the house," he said, "and put something on that. If there's a clean surface in here, I don't see it."

"Neither do I. Don't worry, Abe. I'll be fine."

Not wanting to move away from her, he asked, "How's Pal doing?"

"Better. I've spent several sleepless nights with her, but that's good because she's regaining her strength. She's beginning to lap the milk replacer out of a dish and is thrilled each time I offer her softened dog food. Her tail stops wagging only when she's asleep, but even then her tiny paws twitch. Sometimes she cries out."

"In pain?"

"I don't think so. It's something dogs do, though the sounds bother Buddy. He makes similar noises and motions while sleeping. A K-9 handler I met called the motions and sounds 'chasing rabbits.' Buddy isn't happy unless Pal's box is nearby so he can keep a watchful eye on both of us."

"Is he here?" He looked around the garage that resembled a hoarder's dream.

"No. I left him inside so he wouldn't get hurt."

"And you did instead. What are you doing out here?"

Instead of explaining, she pulled out a folded sheet of bright blue paper and handed it to him. He opened it and read,

"My dearest Jenna,

"When you were young, I told you to stay away from the old garage behind the house. It was filled with tools that had been left by your *grossdawdi* and the man who sold us this property. Do you remember me telling you about him? He fixed cars and other vehicles, and he continued to use the garage, renting it from us.

"You're old enough to be careful in there now, so go in and look in the middle drawer of the work table at the rear. You'll find a wooden box that I discovered when I decided to clean out the garage. I didn't get far, as you'll see. Please deliver the box to the person whose name is on it.

"I know this is no challenge, but I don't want to over-whelm you. Take the time you would have used to de-vise an answer to my clues and use it to enjoy your time in Sweetwater."

It was signed "With love from your *grossmammi*."

"She's made it simple this week." Abe handed the letter to Jenna.

"She tried." She waved a hand at a battered workbench. "The drawer is stuck. It won't move, and I'm afraid if I try again, I'll rip the knob right off it."

"Let me try."

Abe edged past her and grasped the rough wooden knobs on the drawer. He tugged. One flew off in his right hand, while his left palm burned with abrasion when the drawer didn't move. Looking around, he grabbed a crowbar. He slid one end into the side of the drawer.

"Okay?" he asked. "It might ruin the drawer."

"I'm not going to let a single plank keep me from doing as *Grossmammi* Dinah asked."

With a grin, he nodded. He pushed on the crowbar. The

drawer creaked a warning, and the front panel began to split. He gritted his teeth and shoved harder. The lower half of the drawer front flew past him and struck the car with a loud metallic clang.

Jenna stuck her hand in before he could warn her to be careful. Then he wondered why he'd even considered wasting his breath. Jenna Rose Shetler would never wait for common sense. She always went for the quick and simple solution.

She pulled out a wooden box that had a logo for cheese on its sides. The box had to be as ancient as the car because he'd never heard of the company. Setting it on top of the workbench, she slid the wooden top across and looked inside.

"Old spark plugs?" she asked. "*This* is what *Grossmammi* Dinah wanted to go to…" She looked at the box. "To Chuck Carpenter?"

"It would seem so." He leaned the crowbar against the workbench. "There must be a reason as there was with the plates. How many are in there?"

"Five." Putting the spark plug back, she closed the box. "Do you know where Chuck Carpenter lives?"

"I know a Mr. Carpenter who lives near the ocean. I don't know what his first name is."

"Do you remember if he visited my grandmother?"

He shook his head. "Can't say that I do. Shall we go?"

"Why not?" She took a single step. "Oh, let me clean this knee before we go."

"*Gut* idea."

He resisted assisting her as she found her way out of the mess and debris that had fallen from the roof. While she went into the house, he finished emptying and cleaning the pails. He put them back in the barn and was ready to leave by the time she came out of the house, a small white bandage on her knee contrasting with her tan. She carried Pal's box and had Buddy trailing behind her.

They got in the truck and headed south. "Abe, I was wondering if you and the twins would be interested in helping me. I'm retraining Buddy."

"To do what?" He glanced at where the German shepherd was stretched out by the puppy's box in a casual pose. They'd come to what Abe deemed an understanding—they'd ignore one another.

"Find things, people, whatever is lost."

"Can you do that? Train him to do something else?"

She smiled. "For Buddy, finding a special scent is a game. If he finds the item I've hidden, I give him his favorite toy for playtime. He's so strong that when he tugs on the rubber squirrel, I have to fight to keep my balance. To him, it's fun, so he's eager to find the item. He's happy, and I'm happy. He learned how to pick out the odors from bomb components. Now I'm helping him learn to trail after a specific odor I've shared with him."

"Oh, like holding someone's clothing for him to sniff?"

"Exactly. If he traces the scent, it'll bring him to what or who I want him to find. Once he does that, he gets to play." She slowed for a stop sign. "Would you and the twins be interested in helping me create scent trails for Buddy to follow? I can't always be the source because he may assume that's the only scent I want him to track."

"Zeke and Zoe will be thrilled, I know. They'll see it as a different sort of hide-and-seek game."

"Not you?" She turned onto the road after a single car went past.

"I'm not sure I'll have the time you'll need for training Buddy. Work on your *grossmammi*'s farm and at the wood shop is getting busier."

He thought she'd insist, but she said, "I get that. Will you check with the twins? It may be boring for them at first because I don't know how long it'll take Buddy to figure out this new game, but they like him."

Did she think he was a coward? He glanced at his unbending fingers. Buddy hadn't snapped at anyone, but Abe couldn't trust any dog. He knew that bothered Jenna, but he'd been foolish once. He wouldn't be again.

The Carpenter house was a small cottage not far from the Atlantic. It was the very last house on a dead-end road. A line of trees protected it from storm winds, but its paint had been scored away by salt and sunshine. The garage behind it looked new and fresh and as if it'd had a lot more attention than the house. The sounds of small waves lapping the shore were almost drowned out by the raucous calls of gulls and other seabirds.

Jenna drew in a deep breath, savoring the scents of salt and marsh. The house was bucolic in the summer sunshine.

"This is amazing!" She took another deep breath.

Abe came around the truck to gaze over the marsh and the water beyond. "God created stunning vistas, ain't so?"

"Ocean views are my favorite. I wonder what's under the water and what I'll see on it." She got out, bringing the wooden box with her. "Let's find Mr. Carpenter."

Seeing an elderly man with tufts of white hair peeking out around his ears, she walked toward the garage. The pudgy man was shorter than she was, and a bushy white beard gave him the appearance of a mall Santa. His eyes twinkled when he called a greeting.

"Yep," he said in response to Jenna's question if he knew her grandmother. "Dinah was a good friend. We used to go birding together. Somehow, she always managed to discover one or two more species than I did." He tapped his temple and chuckled. "Her old eyes were better than my old eyes."

Jenna held out the narrow wooden box. "My grandmother wanted you to have this."

"A cheese box?" Again he laughed. "To remind me of the sandwiches she always made for our excursions? That was nice of her to remember to include me."

"I don't think it's the box. It's what's in it." She motioned for him to open it.

Mr. Carpenter slid the top. "Well, I'll be. I..." Tears welled up in his eyes as he carried the box to the garage and lifted the door with a little help from Abe.

Jenna stared at the car inside. The honey-colored vehicle gleamed as if it had just come off the production line. "It's beautiful. A Ford Model A, isn't it?"

"It is."

"Did you restore it?"

Mr. Carpenter nodded. "It's taken me almost thirty years to get it to look this good. I'm still working on the engine because there are some parts I haven't been able to find. Not that that's stopped people from trying to buy it, but it'd be like selling my child." He looked at the box he held. "These are rechargeable spark plugs for the car." He patted the antique car beside him.

"You mean they're still usable?" Abe asked.

"Most likely." His smile was sad. "Trust Dinah to know what I needed to finish bringing this old car to life. Once I get the car going, you must let me take you for a ride."

Jenna hurried to say, "You're welcome to come to the farm and see if there's anything else in the garage you can use."

"You're very kind, young lady."

"Just trying to do as *Grossmammi* Dinah would want." She realized she was. Her offer wasn't pretense or an attempt to get more junk out of the garage before the building collapsed on pitted and rusty car parts.

"She'd be proud of you, Jenna."

Warmth coursed into her shattered heart at his kind words. It was followed by a thud of grief. Her eyes turned toward Abe, who stood beside her. Seeing the sorrow in his own gaze, she knew she'd betrayed her thoughts. She waited for a pulse of dismay, but it didn't come. Instead, she was glad he was beside her. It was a moment she'd treasure even after she'd put Sweetwater in her rearview mirror and returned with Buddy back to work.

If she returned…

Where had that thought come from? She silenced it. All her efforts had been concentrated on becoming a K-9 cop again. Nothing—not even the friends she was making in Sweetwater—must get in the way of that dream. She couldn't let Abe distract her from what she must do. As soon as she handled *Grossmammi* Dinah's last letter, she must leave Sweetwater and head back to her interrupted life.

But, all of the sudden, it didn't seem so easy.

Chapter Nine

When Abe arrived to get ready for the evening milking, Jenna was letting Buddy out of the house. She held the screened porch door open, and the dog raced past her toward the tree he'd claimed for his private business. Not so private, because Pal followed...or tried to.

Jenna carried the puppy down the steps. Setting her on the ground, she watched Pal stumble through the grass to Buddy. A week and a half after Jenna had found the pup, Pal was still scrawny and had patches of her black-and-white fur missing, but she seemed to be gaining the strength she should have. Buddy looked back, and Abe could have almost believed the German shepherd sighed. As much as Buddy adored the puppy, he must want privacy.

At that thought, Abe loped across the grass to get Pal. "How about letting Buddy have a moment for himself?" The puppy wiggled until Abe held her so she could see Buddy. She twisted and licked Abe's nose with her tiny, pink tongue.

"That's her way of saying *danki*." Jenna walked over to where he stood.

"You're using *Deitsch* when talking about her. Why? Do you think she's from an Amish puppy mill?"

She recoiled, and he realized his voice had been too hard. Just as it'd been when they were kids, and something she'd said had gotten under his skin. He wasn't that way with anyone else. If he was irritated, he swallowed his annoyance and kept on going. So why couldn't he do the same with her?

Because you want to be honest with her.

He wasn't going to listen to his thoughts. They led him into trouble too often. They brought forth memories of Jenna's smiles and Jenna's laugh and Jenna patching him up when he tumbled and hurt a knee or an elbow. Then, he'd been able to say whatever he wanted, and she was okay.

Don't lie to yourself, came a retort from inside his head. *She wasn't okay the night when she blurted out her feelings for you.*

He didn't want to think of that night, but those memories now drifted through his mind whenever he didn't make an effort to silence them. If he could take back those uncaring words, he would. He'd have retracted them that night. He hated the memory of her face going from joy to horror in the midst of a single breath as laughter burst out of him. Maybe his words hadn't been as painful as the bomb that had taken her leg, but they'd been as devastating. For years, he'd put that night into a locked corner of his memory. Now it refused to stay silent.

Asking forgiveness was something he should have done long ago. "Jenna, I'm—"

"I don't know where Pal is from, but she's home with Buddy and me. The twins speak to her in *Deitsch,* so I thought… Never mind. It was a stupid joke."

He'd let this go on too long. "I'm sorry, Jenna. I know you've been worried about Pal. I should have been more understanding."

"You should have." She held out her hands and gathered the puppy close. Pal nuzzled her as if Jenna were the *boppli*'s *mamm,* and Jenna swaddled her with her palms. "I could use some iced tea. Emphasis on the ice. How about you?"

"Sounds *gut.*"

"C'mon. You can sit on the porch with Pal while I get us some glasses." She raised her voice. "Buddy, I'm going inside."

Abe sighed as he sat on one of the rockers. The constant whir of insects was no longer in his ears on the screened porch. Dinah had inspected the screen several times each summer, determined to keep bugs off her porch. He added it to his job list for the farm. No need to bother Jenna with it. She had enough to do with fulfilling her *grossmammi*'s wishes.

Thanking Jenna when she handed him an already sweating glass, he took an appreciative drink as she sat in the other chair after putting another glass and a pitcher on the table beside her. "This is the life," he mused. "Sitting and rocking and enjoying God's beautiful bounty."

"It does have its appeal."

"Much better than in the city with its crowds and honking horns, ain't so?"

"That has its appeal, too."

His heart faltered, surprising him. Why was it acting so oddly? Jenna had made it clear from the day she returned that she'd leave once she'd completed the task Dinah had given her. He took another deep drink of the tea to cover his sigh. He shouldn't forget she was a city woman, despite the fact he'd known her as a country kid running around the fields in bare feet. When she'd arrive with fancy clothing and gear each year, it'd taken her a week or two to push it aside and wear the simpler clothing Dinah collected from yard sales and thrift stores.

He knew pushing the subject would be useless. "One thing I've been thinking about. Why didn't Dinah create a living trust?"

"If she had, there wouldn't have been an executor." She chuckled. "We wouldn't be having fun with her letters."

He heard her sarcasm but he ignored it. "Fun may not be the exact term I'd choose, but Dinah is keeping herself in your life, ain't so?"

Her hand froze with her glass halfway to her mouth. Lowering it, she gripped her bottom lip with her teeth. To keep it from trembling? She looked away, but he was certain he'd seen the sudden glitter of tears in her eyes. He wanted to put his arms around her and offer what scanty comfort he could as she mourned for her *grossmammi*, the woman she'd adored and who had given her an escape from her crazy family.

Just as Dinah had offered him a way to spend time away from his own indifferent parents and chaotic siblings.

He was beginning to realize how vast their shared loss was.

The Saturday afternoon was perfect for training, though Jenna and Buddy had practiced their searches while he learned to sniff for bombs in rain and snow and bone-gnawing cold. This morning, the air was fresh for the last weekend in June. She guessed the afternoon would bring more smothering humidity.

Buddy was enjoying Pal chasing him, nipping at his feathered tail. The German shepherd bounced about as if he were no older than the pup until Jenna brought out his training leash, which extended twenty feet. Together the two dogs crisscrossed the field, following the scent she'd laid down last night.

When Buddy found a sock she'd hidden deep in the corn crib amongst rotting kernels, she praised him and gave him five minutes of play. Then she had to give Pal some attention. Both dogs regarded her with tongues lolling, eager for their next search. They'd already found three out of the four items she'd hidden.

She unlatched his leash, then offered the scent she'd sprayed on the cloth she held and the other sock. Buddy sniffed it, then tested the air. Pal tried to do the same and sneezed. With a laugh, she patted their heads before motioning for Buddy to begin. He'd already learned that when she took him off the leash, it meant she wanted him to search in a building.

They ran into the loafing shed while she set her stopwatch.

At this distance, Buddy needed to be able to trace the scent to its source in less than ten minutes.

"What are they doing?" asked Zeke as he ran to where she stood.

"Working."

"Dogs work?" Zoe shielded her eyes with her hand, squinting to see the dogs in the shadows.

Jenna took the twins by the hand and led them to the house. "Buddy works. Pal is copying everything Buddy does."

"Like Zoe does with me." Zeke nodded his head.

His twin scowled. "Like Zeke does with *me*."

She had to stop a debate neither would win. "Buddy has found one sock. Now he's searching for the other one."

"Why?"

She sat on the edge of the porch beside the twins, but kept an eye on her dogs who were circling the shed, following the scent trail.

"Because someday," she said with a smile, "Buddy and Pal may be able to help someone who's lost."

"Like hide-and-seek?" Zoe asked.

"I like hide-and-seek!" Zeke jumped off the porch.

Jenna caught his sleeve and halted him from careening after the dogs. "It's not hide-and-seek. It's—" She didn't want to say "life and death." The words might upset the youngsters. "It's called search and rescue. Did Abe tell you I could use your help with training Buddy?"

"*Ja,*" they said together.

Giving them quick instructions, she had them rub their hands on a washcloth before they raced in the opposite direction of where Buddy was beginning to bark. It was his signal he'd found something, and it had been the most difficult part of his training because when he'd discovered a suspected bomb, he'd sat and was silent. Nobody wanted a bouncy, barking dog setting off an explosive device by mistake.

She praised Buddy and Pal, gave them their playing time and put Buddy on his leash. She offered him the washcloth with the children's scents. It was a new challenge. Following two different trails.

She wasn't sure how useful the twins would be because she could hear them giggling before Buddy raced forward to where they sat under a tree. Then she realized searching for a person wasn't like trying to locate a bomb. If someone who was lost heard them, the person would shout to them.

Next time, she'd make it clearer to the kids that they needed to be in separate places, but Buddy had proved he would follow a scent other than hers.

"You did a great job," she told all four. After playing with the dogs, she pulled a pair of candy bars out of her pocket. The twins tore off the covering as she said, "Next time we do this training with Buddy, I don't want you to make a sound until he licks your face. Do you think you can do that?"

"I can." Zeke hooked a thumb toward his sister as they walked toward the house. "She can't. She's always talking."

Jenna smiled. Both twins chattered like squirrels. Instead of saying that, she asked, "Do you want to try?"

"*Ja!*" they shouted as they sprinted away.

She realized why when she saw Abe in the yard. The twins raced toward him. He looked past them to her, and she felt as if the distance between them had vanished. As if it was just the two of them beneath the bright blue summer sky. That sensation lasted less than a second, but the golden warmth imprinted itself on her heart in a way she hadn't expected.

Somehow, she was able to say, as she reached where Abe stood with the twins, "Okay, now you can play with Buddy." Bending toward the kids, she wagged her finger. "No more attempts to get him to swing on the tire."

The twins looked guilty before Zoe said, "Buddy wants to swing with us, ain't so? Ain't so, Abe?"

He gave her an indulgent smile, but his words were stern. "Jenna knows Buddy better than we do. We need to listen to her."

"Can Pal play, too?" Zeke asked.

"If she wants to," Jenna replied, "but she's a baby, and she's been running around for an hour. She may want to take a nap."

Pal showed no signs of exhaustion as she joined Buddy in chasing after the children, but soon the puppy lagged behind.

Jenna watched while Zoe knelt and leaned Pal's chin on her shoulder. "They are being gentle with her."

"They're used to being the littlest ones," Abe said, "and knowing how hard it is to keep up with everyone else."

"You're going to miss them when they start school."

"They're just five, so they've got to wait until next year to become scholars." He clasped his hands as he looked at her. "You're right. I'm going to miss them a lot, though I've got to admit I'm looking forward to completing a task without being interrupted a dozen times."

"You're exaggerating."

"All right, a half dozen times." He grinned. "Except for the times when they interrupt me more than a dozen times."

Jenna pretended to be worried about the puppy so she didn't have to meet Abe's eyes. The image of him, wrapped in golden sunshine, lingered. She was thrown back in time to her last summer in Sweetwater when she'd become aware of him in a different way. Everything in her life had changed since then. Why did she continue to be attracted to him? He'd told her point-blank, years ago, that she was silly to love him. She had been. What had she known about life then?

So why couldn't she forget how much she'd wanted to spend even more time with him then…and now?

A sharp crack of sound followed by a shriek lacerated her thoughts. A fierce barking. Another detonation. Shouts…

The world collapsed around her again, but this time into fire-laced darkness. Pain. Sharp pain. Pain unlike any she'd ever felt. Not from her leg but from knowing she'd failed her partner.

No!

Stop it!

It's over!

It wasn't. It was beginning again. She couldn't stop the time-out. Not even knowing Abe and the twins were there made an iota of difference. The next wave of pain and grief and guilt rolled her off her feet, sending her to drown in what she couldn't change or forget, no matter how hard she'd tried.

She was failing again.

Abe watched color fade from Jenna's face. She clutched her arms to herself as she cried out for her dog. Buddy raced toward her as she wobbled. Not caring if the dog attacked him, Abe rushed forward and wrapped his arms around Jenna as she sank to the ground. How many times had he imagined holding her? He'd lost count, but he knew not a single one of those dreams had been like this.

She fought to get away and screamed for Buddy. The twins stared in horror and disbelief as she sobbed and thrashed, fighting him in an effort to escape.

Escape what? She was too incoherent to ask. He heard his brother and sister shouting questions. He ignored them, other than motioning with his head toward the house. He didn't want them to get kicked as she was doing to him. When they hesitated, he shouted for them to go.

They ran, but neither dog followed them, in spite of them calling to Buddy and Pal. The German shepherd stared at his partner and moaned deep in his throat. Pal inched closer, but Buddy pushed her away.

Abe was grateful. He couldn't risk letting go of Jenna long enough to get the puppy out of her reach. Her flailing fists pounded his back as he kept her from hurting herself. He'd seen an epileptic seizure one time. This was similar, but her motions weren't erratic. They were aimed at inflicting as much pain as possible so she could escape.

Then she sagged to the ground. She whimpered as if she were as broken as Pal had been. Her fists dropped, and her fingers unfolded like dying butterflies. Buddy stuck his snout between her and Abe. A single lick on her face was, Abe guessed, the dog's way of letting her know he hadn't deserted her.

Slowly her eyes opened, and she gazed at him. Pain and humiliation mixed in them. "I'm sorry, Abe," she whispered.

"What do you have to be sorry for?" He helped her sit, making sure she wouldn't tumble to the grass again.

"That you had to see me like this."

He cupped her chin and tilted her face toward him. It wasn't easy to ignore the streaks where tears had scorched her cheeks. "I'd be happy never to have to watch you endure such pain again, Jenna, but you don't have anything to apologize for. Are you okay?"

"I will be. It takes a few hours for everything to wear off. I—" She looked past him as a car door slammed.

The Rickaboughs crossed the yard. Abe wanted to groan, because the last thing Jenna needed was to be pestered by her demanding cousins. He started to tell her he'd deal with them, but she silenced him by putting a quivering hand on his arm.

"What's going on here?" asked Daryl, frowning.

"Nothing now." Jenna swiped her hand across her cheeks, then pushed herself to stand along with Abe. She swayed, but waved aside his hand. "I fell, and Abe was kind enough to make sure I wasn't injured."

It wasn't a lie, but it wasn't the truth. Abe kept his mouth shut, knowing she didn't want her cousins to know what had happened. What *had* happened? Why had she cried out and toppled over, fighting to get away from him?

With a yelp, Pal pushed her way past them and stared at her

cousins. Pal crouched, her head bent as she began to make soft mewling cries. Buddy growled and used his snout to shove the puppy aside again, this time farther from the Rickaboughs. Jenna took her, and Pal buried her face in the curve of Jenna's elbow, trying to shut out the world.

Her cousins scowled, and Daryl asked, "You've got *another* dog?"

Geneva swore and took a single step forward. She halted when Buddy rumbled a warning deep in his throat. "How many more are you going to bring into Dinah's house?" She shot a glance at Daryl.

Abe was unsure what that look was supposed to convey, but Daryl did. "We'll never get the reek of them out of here after we move in."

"My dogs don't stink." Jenna's voice was hard, but her fingers shook as she cradled the pup.

Abe kept his hand behind her, not touching her, but ready to catch her if she wobbled. She'd be mortified to show any helplessness to her cousins.

The Rickaboughs didn't stay long. They asked the same questions about Dinah's will as they did each week. When they finally accepted that Jenna had nothing new to tell them, they drove out, the tires spewing gravel in their wake.

"Let's get you to where you can sit." Abe put his hand on her lower back to guide her toward the house.

"I'm okay. Now." She released a long breath. "Daryl is getting worse. Doesn't he realize no matter how often he asks me for information I don't have the answer is always going to be the same?"

Abe didn't reply. Instead he helped her into the house, shooed the twins out, made sure the dogs had food and water and returned to the living room where she was lying on the sofa with her eyes closed. She admitted to a headache, but told him it would go away soon.

"It's always the same," she murmured. "I should be grateful I'm alive. If this is the price I have to pay—"

"God isn't punishing you."

"How do you know?" She opened her eyes and met his.

"Because He's a loving Father, and He wants the best for His *kinder.*" He knelt by the sofa. "*Komm* to church with us tomorrow. It's at the Glicks'. Sass would be delighted for you to join us." He added when she opened her mouth to answer, "If you don't want to attend our service, I understand. You're welcome to join us afterward."

"Mr. Carpenter asked me to go to the Sweetwater Bible Church with him, and I told him I would." She took his hand and folded it between her smaller ones. "Thank you, Abe. For asking and for…for everything."

He wanted to leave his hand in hers, but had to withdraw it when he heard the twins calling his name. Their voices were a reminder of the world he belonged to and how different it was from the world she belonged to.

It was something he couldn't allow himself to forget again, even though his heart begged him to.

Chapter Ten

Avoiding Elden after the church service on Sunday so Abe didn't have to discuss why he hadn't accomplished anything with the youth group yet was easier than he'd expected. *God, danki for understanding that Your servant is trying his best.* He wasn't sure how to explain that his plan depended on Jenna, and she'd agreed reluctantly to go to the meeting. However, she still insisted the teens wouldn't heed what she had to say.

"None of them that should listen," she'd amended the last time they'd spoken about a time and place for a get-together for the youth. "They don't have any reason to heed a single word you say, so you've got to get their attention."

She was right. He knew that, but no inspiration had pointed him at another way of approaching the problem. He'd hoped to convince her to join the teens on Saturday night during a volleyball gathering at his house. She'd been at his house many times as a kid, so it would be familiar territory for her. Or it should be—he couldn't be sure how much she remembered of the rambling house that his parents had added on to with each additional *boppli*.

But she had said that would be a bad idea because the kids wouldn't want to be lectured when they were attending to have a *gut* time. He needed to—

His thoughts were interrupted by a familiar laugh and a bark. He stared across the Glicks' backyard to see Jenna talking with Sass, who was petting Buddy with one hand while she held Pal with the other. When he saw Jenna glancing toward the plain teens, who were wandering away to a nearby school where they could play baseball, he wondered if she'd timed her visit when they would be gone. So many times when he and Jenna were kids, she'd arrived after a church Sunday's midday meal and joined in with the baseball game.

He made his way over to Jenna and Sass, and exchanged greetings. Sass gave Pal a gentle squeeze, then handed her to Jenna before saying she needed to check something in the kitchen. A quick glance around the yard told him nobody else was going to encroach on them.

"Jenna—"

"Somewhere else," she hissed and pushed past him.

Surprised, he watched her walk toward her truck. She had something to tell him, something she didn't want others to overhear.

He leaned one elbow on her truck and watched her lift Pal into the back. The pup curled on a blanket, falling asleep. Buddy did the same beside Jenna.

"I want to explain," she said. "About yesterday and the time-out."

"Time-out?" His brows tilted. "Isn't that a punishment *Englischers* give to their *kinder* when they've been naughty?"

"Yes-s-s." She drew out the word.

"So do you think you need to be punished by having these bad times?"

"No, of course not!"

He arched a single brow.

She mirrored his motion back at him. "You don't understand what I'm dealing with."

"You're right. I don't understand. How can I—or anyone other than Buddy—understand when you keep this to yourself?"

"It's not something I like to talk about."

"Maybe, or is it something you're ashamed of?"

Abe's words sliced into Jenna's heart as if he'd slammed a knife into her chest. That might have been easier to deal with because he would have spared her from having to answer the unanswerable. Now she stood facing him, his eyes offering her sanctuary at the same time they pleaded for her to be honest with him.

She opened her mouth to respond, but wasn't sure how to reply. With the truth? The awful truth of her failures, which had led to disaster? Or should she cling to the half-truths she'd shared with the police psychiatrist and her superiors and even herself? The half-truths that served her so well... most of the time.

He remained as still as she was. Nobody else had been so patient. Everyone, including the psychiatrist, had found the silence uncomfortable, even threatening. Noticing that Abe's lips were moving, she realized he was praying.

Praying for her. Could his prayers reach God when He had ignored hers?

"I'm tired, Abe." The words slipped out before she could halt him. "Not tired like I haven't slept. Just tired."

"Of what?"

"Of hiding the truth from everyone." She shivered as she leaned against the truck. "Of hiding it from myself."

"Tell me."

"Yesterday..."

"Yesterday something happened we need to talk about." He moved his hand so it was less than a finger's breadth from her shoulder. While the rest of the members of his church were gathered in the yard, he wouldn't get any closer.

She wasn't sure if she was happy about that or distressed. She didn't want to have to depend on anyone for strength, but his arms around her would be the rampart she needed to hold back the battle within her.

"It's called a flashback," she said. "It used to happen a lot when something triggered it."

"Something like...?"

"Did a car backfire just before someone screamed?"

He nodded. "*Ja.* I heard something from the main road at the same time Zoe shouted for Zeke to make her go higher on the swing." He regarded her with astonishment. "Something so commonplace as those sounds can—what did you call it?"

"Trigger a flashback. Yes, they can. In fact, that's what causes an episode. I can be prepared for something extraordinary, but I can't be on guard every second."

His fingertip brushed her upper arm. It was a simple motion, yet it offered comfort only Buddy had been able to give her before. A comfort that was filled with empathy and the longing to make the pain vanish. How could Abe do that with a simple touch?

"Is there anything I can do to help?" he asked, and her heart urged her to forget the onlookers and throw her arms around him to thank him for his kindness.

"I wish there was. I wish there was something *I* could do. I don't get any warning. When the time-out begins, it's like I'm here and there at the same time."

His eyes narrowed, and she knew he was trying to grasp what she wasn't explaining well. "There? Where the bomb went off?"

"Yes." She wrapped her arms around herself. "I can see the pattern of the shop doors and the displays in the windows. I can hear people talking. Not customers. Other cops. There was another K-9 bomb-sniffing team in the mall. Also I can hear the commander's voice from my radio. Everything from the smooth floor under my feet to the odors from the food court are real." She shifted, her fingers unclenching before she locked them together. "I know it's not real. I mean, I know now is now and that was then. It's like a movie I can't stop. I can't change anything. I have to live it again before I can escape."

"I had no idea." He sighed.

"I know." With a sigh of her own, she added, "That's the usual time-out. It's worse sometimes because I see Buddy vanish, and I don't know if he's alive or dead. Everything gets blurry like chalk in the rain. Then I ask what I did so wrong that I can't escape this torment. I pray and I pray for it to go away, but it doesn't."

He stepped in front of her and put his hands on her shoulders. "I've told you I believe God is a loving Father who watches His *kinder* make mistakes and is filled with joy when they learn from them, so He doesn't have to weep with them when they make the same mistake again."

"Just different ones?"

He gave her the faintest smile. "Some of us learn the easy way. Some of us have to have tough lessons before it sinks through our thick heads."

"I'm in the latter group."

"Me, too." He opened the rear gate of her truck. As easily as if she were no bigger than one of the twins, he lifted her to sit on the tailgate. He sat beside her. "If you don't want to tell me today—or any time in the future—any more than this, I'll have to accept that. If you don't want to tell me today, but at some other time about what happened, I'll be glad to listen. You used to listen to my heartaches when I was young. It's time I repaid you."

"You listened to my whining then, too."

He tapped her on the nose before Buddy pushed his way between them. He smiled as she draped her arm over her protective partner. "You, Jenna Rose Shetler, have never whined. Not once in your life. You may have complained. You may have threatened to raise a ruckus, but not once have I heard you whine."

"Then you weren't listening."

He leaned toward her across Buddy, so near she couldn't see anything but his kind eyes. "Jenna, I've heard every word you've spoken to me. Sometimes, I didn't let on because you were an annoying pest at times—"

"I wasn't annoying." She cocked an eyebrow at him. "I was always adorable. That's what my grandmother said."

"We know what a smart woman Dinah was, but that doesn't change that you were as pesky as a skeeter at times."

She smiled, grateful how he was lighting her way out of the shadows left in the aftermath of her time-out. "Thank you." She flung her arms around his shoulders and, stretching across Buddy who lowered himself to the truck's bed, pressed her face to his shirt.

Good sense burst through her, and she jerked away. Her face was burning as she told him she was sorry. Not only had she breached the wall that must remain between them, but she had done so in public. Would the bishop chastise him? If so, she was ready to explain her spontaneous reaction to Abe's gentle, consoling words.

"You don't need to apologize, Jenna." He glanced past her, clearly anxious to see if anyone had witnessed their inappropriate hug. "We're friends. We've always been friends, and I hope that doesn't change."

"Me, too." It wasn't the truth. For the brief moment—no longer than a single heartbeat—when she'd had her arms around him, she'd discovered she'd never gotten over her crush on Abe Bontranger.

Had Richard sensed that? How many times had he accused her of thinking less about him than the other aspects of her life? She'd always assumed he meant her work, but what if he'd known her heart could never belong to him?

Now he was gone, and Abe couldn't be a part of her life other than as the friend he was telling her he must be.

She didn't feel bad about Richard, but she couldn't imagine living the rest of her life without Abe. Yet she must figure out how to do that.

Jenna was beginning to believe she could set her watch by the arrival of the mail. She waved to the mail carrier as his small truck was pulling away from the mailbox. Taking out this week's letter, she stared at it and sighed.

Buddy leaned against her right side, offering her comfort. He had been extraprotective of her since the time-out on Saturday.

Ruffling the hair between his ears, she smiled at him. "What do you think? Another easy one, or did *Grossmammi* Dinah devise an even more obscure way of telling me what she wants me to do next?"

He gave a single bark and wagged his tail.

"I appreciate your support, Buddy, but I'm hoping we don't need to put our thinking caps on for this one."

Tilting his head, he looked at her before heading to the house at his top speed. Jenna understood his hurry when, as she approached the steps, she heard a faint yip from inside.

She opened the door and let Buddy bolt past her. Who could have guessed her partner had such a paternal side? After he nosed the puppy, as if checking her for any changes since leaving Pal indoors less than two minutes ago, Buddy dropped to the floor with a contented sigh. The puppy clambered over him and nipped at his ears. Buddy accepted it with aplomb.

Jenna went into the kitchen and lifted the remnants of her midmorning snack from the top of the fridge. She'd made the mistake of leaving a piece of toast and jam on the table unguarded yesterday. Pal had eaten part of it and tracked the raspberry jam and toast crumbs through the whole ground floor.

She took a bite and sat at the table where she had a good view of the front door. It seemed odd not to have Abe with her while she read the letter. Feeling as if she were doing something wrong, though the letter was addressed to her, she opened the envelope and pulled out an orange sheet of paper. It was so bright in the morning sunshine, she had to blink to look at it. She shifted in her chair, so the page wasn't bathed in the light from the window.

Dear, dear Jenna,
Do you remember my favorite verse from the fifth chapter of Galatians? It's the twenty-second verse. The fruit of the Spirit is love, joy, peace, longsuffering, gentleness, goodness, faith. *It's a verse you heard me say often. That's because it was embossed on my heart by God's love.*

But you don't want to read an old woman's ramblings, ain't so? Make sure Daryl takes those rusty tools out of the loafing shed. If he can't use them, he can sell them for scrap. You don't need them out there where someone could get hurt. Knowing your dog and Abe's little brother and sister, I'm sure they're curious what's out there. Three noses sticking in among those tools could lead to trouble...and stitches.

Jenna chuckled. The twins and the dogs had been in the loafing shed in recent days. When had the letter been written? Months ago, she guessed. Yet it was as if her grandmother was standing right there and making an amusing observation. Her laugh faded when she wondered how Daryl would respond to another mention of him in *Grossmammi* Dinah's will but not about the farm.

Not well. She reread the verse from Galatians. *Grossmammi* Dinah had told her long-suffering meant patience. Not just with waiting for something Jenna wanted, but with getting through difficult situations or dealing with contrary people without losing hope and faith and her temper. It hadn't been an easy lesson to grasp, but it had served her well as a police officer.

She sighed. It wasn't a lesson Daryl had taken to heart. In fact, he seemed determined to bully her into giving him answers she didn't have. She wondered how long she could keep from telling him that people far more threatening than him had tried to intimidate her. They'd failed, and so would he.

She pushed aside those thoughts as *Grossmammi* Dinah's voice warning about not abusing the fruits of the spirit echoed in her head. She must practice forbearance if she expected Daryl to do the same. For now, she wanted to finish reading the precious letter from her grandmother and see what puzzle she needed to solve this week. She couldn't hope for another straightforward letter.

> *Are you comfortable in the house? When you visited, it took you the better part of a month to shrug off the hurry-hurry-hurry life you lived with your* mamm *and to slow to Sweetwater time. Savoring time marked by the ticktock of a clock while you sit on the front porch and watch the sun chasing shadows across the lawn.*
>
> *I hope you haven't forgotten the Art of listening to the bugs' singing and the whispers of rain through the leaves. Don't forget to listen to the clock instead of watching it.*
>
> *Think about this, Jenna, and you'll have your answer for this week: Do All Messages Exactly Right, Okay.*
>
> *Have fun,* liebling. *If you need help, look in the barn. You'll find what you seek there if you are open to God's blessings.*

As always it was signed "With love."

She turned over the page, but it was blank. Was that the

whole message? She wasn't even sure what part was supposed to be a clue to this week's bequest.

Then she noticed some of the words were oddly capitalized and put them together.

A D A M E R O

Was it a word? If so, it wasn't one she knew. Maybe it was an anagram, the letters mixed up. She played with the letters, rearranging them, but couldn't figure out anything that made sense.

What if the word was *Deitsch*? It was her grandmother's first language. *Deitsch* was a spoken language, and the same word could be spelled in many different ways.

She folded the letter and put it in the envelope. She'd keep an eye out for Abe. Maybe he'd see something she hadn't.

"*Grossmammi* Dinah," she said to the empty kitchen, "I know you wanted to make this challenging for me. Why?"

She stared at the stove as her own question echoed through the kitchen. Could that be the reason for her grandmother's peculiar will? Joyce Allgyer had mentioned the will was something *Grossmammi* Dinah had thought would be fun. Had her grandmother guessed how desperate Jenna was to return to real police work, so *Grossmammi* Dinah decided to give Jenna a chance to play detective with the clues in her letters?

With her hands over her face, she leaned her elbows on the table. "Oh, my!" she breathed out, realizing she might have set this whole situation into motion.

Buddy growled, and Pal bumbled into the kitchen, cowering near Jenna's feet. Standing, she called to her partner. Buddy stayed between her and Pal. She looked past him, not surprised to see the Rickaboughs.

Daryl strode in. "Anything?"

Not even a hello. Just a one-word demand.

Resisting the urge to give him a single word answer, she shook her head. "Nothing about the farm this week. Though she did mention you."

"A bequest?" asked Geneva, a smile blossoming. "About time."

Jenna focused her cool stare on her cousin's wife. Daryl was the most impatient person in the world, but Geneva rubbed Jenna the wrong way every time she opened her mouth. It might have to do with the fact Geneva made no secret about how she despised dogs. If Buddy was within two yards of her, Geneva pulled her clothes in tight as if she feared some sort of appalling dog cooties would get on her. That Buddy returned Geneva's dislike was no surprise. Her partner was an accurate judge of people.

Daryl flinched as Buddy's growl deepened. "Your dog is a menace."

"He won't hurt you." Jenna used her most calming tone. "He'll attack only if I tell him to."

"You'd better not order him to." Geneva's face was ashen.

"I won't. Do you want to hear about the bequest?"

When they nodded, Jenna read the pertinent part of the letter out loud.

Geneva's smile vanished. "Old metal? What do we want that for?"

"It's going to have some value." Daryl rubbed his hands together. "We can sell it at the scrap yard. Finally something worth something."

They ignored Jenna as they walked out of the kitchen, already planning on how they'd spend the money they'd make from selling the scrap.

She sank to sit at the table again. Putting her arm around Buddy, she stretched to pat Pal. "Two more letters. Let's pray the next one reveals what *Grossmammi* Dinah wants done with the farm. Then we won't have to endure those two any longer."

Buddy licked her face, and she smiled. What would she do without him? She didn't even want to imagine.

Just as she couldn't envision a life without Abe in it, but in two weeks, she'd have to face that future.

Her cell phone rang, and she stared at the screen. Her supervisor. Captain Gould. With a shaky finger, she pressed the screen to answer it.

"Hi, Vic," she said.

"How's the good life treating you, Shetler?"

"Dealing with my grandmother's estate." She was eager to get the pleasantries over with and focus on why she'd contacted him. "Vic, I'm retraining Buddy. He's learning to do search and rescue. Outdoors and in buildings. He's—"

Those were the last words she got in before the call was over less than a minute later. Vic had been succinct. Buddy had been retired, and there was no place for him on the force. Jenna should take her time recovering so she could return to her assignment—her *desk* assignment—when she was finished with *Grossmammi* Dinah's estate. No mention of working on the streets again. No hope for having Buddy as her partner ever again.

Her hopes. Her prayers. For nothing.

"God," she cried from the empty spot in her heart where her dreams had been to the emptiness of the house, "why haven't You listened to my prayers?"

She didn't get an answer, and she no longer expected one.

Chapter Eleven

Jenna balanced the sound-cancelling headphones in her hands two days later. Would they be enough to give her the protection she needed? She looked at the box. On it was printed: "Cancels 90% of noise."

Ninety percent wasn't one hundred, and were the blast and thud of fireworks part of the "most noise" that was muted? She glanced through the dining room window at the sky. The Independence Day sun was sliding toward the west, its path unimpeded by a single cloud. Her hope that a storm would come in off the sea or from across the bay and force the Sweetwater fireworks to be postponed was futile. The night would be as cloudless as the day had been.

She grimaced as she wondered if the humidity and heat would continue after the sun set. It would be cooler in the cellar, but while Abe had rigged a banister and replaced the missing step, she didn't trust herself to navigate the rickety stairs.

Putting the headphones over her ears and turning them on, she ordered Buddy to bark. He jumped to his feet, thinking she was creating a new game. When she again made the motion for him to bark, he obeyed.

The sound reached right through the headphones, muffled but loud enough for her to discern it without straining.

She pulled them off, pushed her humidity-frizzed hair away from her eyes and set the headphones on the table. Would they be enough to protect her from a time-out slamming into her when the fireworks exploded? Even if they were, how was she going to protect Buddy from the noise? She glanced toward the cellar door. They might have to risk it.

Buddy barked again, his tail wagging.

"Good boy." She ruffled his fur when he leaned against her right side. Smiling into his dark eyes, she knew she wasn't fooling him. His posture told her that. He was trying to comfort her, not wanting her to feel anything but happiness. She yearned for the same for him.

And for Abe.

That thought surprised her. Wasn't Abe happy? He had a loving family, and he knew who he was and his strong faith carried him over the bumps in life—everything she wanted for herself, but had no idea how to obtain. Just as she had no idea how to solve the mystery in *Grossmammi* Dinah's latest letter. She'd puzzled over it since its arrival on Tuesday. She'd shown it to Abe when he came over to do the evening chores, and he'd been as stumped as she was. "Clueless about the clues" had been his comment. She'd tried to smile, knowing he was trying to make her feel better, but it'd been impossible.

Taking the letter from the pocket of her shorts, she reread it after letting Buddy outside. Nothing in the letter triggered an answer. What had *Grossmammi* Dinah intended to convey?

"Let's go."

Jenna flinched at Abe's voice, shocked he had come into the house and walked right behind her without her hearing him. Her senses must be getting lazy and dull. Maybe Captain Gould was right to keep her on desk duty. She looked into Abe's gray eyes that were framed by his wire-rimmed glasses. "Go? Where?"

He tapped the headphones box. "I've got a better solution than those."

She folded the letter and put it in her pocket. "For...?"

"For a *gut* way to watch the fireworks."

"Abe, I don't think I should—"

He framed her face with his work-worn hands. His voice was as gentle and as firm as his touch. "Jenna, you used to trust me. If you never trust me again, trust me today."

She bit back her automatic response that she could handle the situation on her own. What a joke that was! She'd depended—and continued to depend—on Buddy. When she was a child, she'd depended on *Grossmammi* Dinah. As her world had expanded during her summers in Sweetwater, she'd depended on Abe. She'd been able to depend on him then, so she'd try to do so again.

"All right," she whispered.

"*Gut*." He lowered his hands, and she ached to grasp them and press them back to her cheeks. "I remember how you always grabbed the best seat for fireworks."

"That was before."

"You still like them, ain't so?"

"In still photographs. Not in real life." She glanced at the door where Buddy was looking through the screen. "I'm not sure how they're going to affect Buddy."

"*Komm* with me." He held out his hand to her.

She placed hers on his palm and watched his fingers close over hers. Neither of them spoke as he grabbed two leashes off the hooks by the door and led her out onto the back porch with Pal romping at their feet. Buddy stepped aside, for once not reacting to Abe touching her.

Jenna almost asked where they were going, but didn't want to give him any reason to release her hand. A peace she hadn't known since her last summer in Sweetwater when she and Abe had talked about everything and nothing washed over her like a calming breeze.

They walked toward the trees along the river. The silence was broken by peepers and birds overhead. He continued to hold her hand as he said, "We need to hurry if we're going to get there on time."

"Where?" Jenna couldn't help asking.

"You'll see."

She'd had enough cryptic comments, but she silently carried Pal because the undergrowth was tall enough to give the puppy trouble.

They stopped at the river. Its black waters had fascinated Jenna as a child. Now she knew the color came from the cypress trees along the river and in the water. The majestic trees with their twisting branches grew wide at the base, creating the knees that offered shelter for small animals.

A boat rocked at a pier that had the raw appearance of freshly cut wood. "Where's the old pier?" she asked. The last time she'd seen it, there had been no boards between the pilings.

"Right here." Abe smiled. "I fixed it."

They stepped out onto the pier. The puppy wiggled harder. Her tongue flicked in every direction in her eagerness to connect with someone. With a smile, Jenna held her out so Pal could leave a long trail of spit on Abe's face. He grimaced, but his eyes were bright with amusement as he wiped his face.

The wood bow of the boat shone in the setting sun as if the golden light came from it. Two rows of seats were upholstered in bright red vinyl with white piping along the edges. The steering wheel was at the front and a large outboard motor, like a sentinel guarding the boat from interlopers, at the stern.

"*Grossmammi* Dinah would have approved of the color of your seats." Jenna chuckled.

"She did. I showed her some sample fabrics, and she urged me to get this one because I'd always be able to pick out my boat from others."

Looking at the empty river, she said, "That doesn't seem to be a problem."

"Do you want to take a ride?"

"Where?"

"You'll see." He gave her a grin that sent warmth to the very tips of her toes.

Nodding, Jenna helped Buddy into the boat. She sat next to him with the puppy on her lap. Untying the boat, Abe jumped in and slipped behind the wheel. He started the motor, moving into the center of the river.

The water was smooth, with few ripples to ruin the reflection of the twilight sky. Along the shores, a few birds were calling their good-nights, and bats were flapping overhead, chasing bugs and creating a stunning pattern that would have enhanced any quilt. When lightning bugs appeared beneath the trees and then disappeared back among the leaves, Pal watched.

"You have another dog who wants to learn search and rescue," Abe said.

Jenna shook her head. "Pal is a border collie. She wants to herd the fireflies. Dogs follow their natural instincts, though they're generous enough to let us train them to use those natural instincts."

"Because you make it into the promise of a special treat for them."

"We're motivated by what makes us feel good. When we had a successful search, whether in training or in the field, I always got a lot of satisfaction out of a job well done." She smiled at Buddy who was sniffing as if he could sample every possible smell along the river. "Buddy got some special playtime."

"Right then?"

Jenna laughed. "You haven't seen ridiculous until you see me and Buddy playing with his rubber squirrel at the same time the bomb squad is making its plans next to us. Far enough away from the bomb so we don't set it off, of course."

"Of course," he said, then chuckled.

The boat put-putted downstream past clumps of trees and then an open field or a house before the trees closed in again. Each time they emerged from under the trees, the sky was several shades darker.

The first stars were poking through the navy blue sky when Abe said, "I'm glad Buddy got into the boat. I wasn't sure if he'd be willing."

"He's a good boy." She stroked her partner's head. "I don't know how the fireworks will affect him. Pal may be enough to keep him distracted, but I can't be sure. Pal may be frightened of the noise, too. Lots of animals who haven't endured what Buddy has are terrified of fireworks."

"What bothers you doesn't seem to bother him or vice versa."

"You've noticed that?"

He smiled. "I've noticed a lot of things about you two. Like how he leans against you often. Not to keep his balance, but to help you keep yours."

"It's that obvious?"

"To someone who knows you well and wants to get to know you better."

Familiar heat climbed her face as she averted her eyes. If she looked into his, would she see the same uncertainty and longing she was experiencing? He'd already told her anything but the most casual friendship between them could cause him trouble. She was a cop, and that was all she'd ever wanted to be. He was Amish, something he had no intention of changing.

They'd reached a stalemate, and neither of them could do anything but lose.

In the tiny hamlet of Rehobeth, about eight miles down the river, Abe drew the boat in next to some pilings near the town's boat ramp. Tying the boat to one of the pilings, he edged it around so his passengers could climb out onto the graveled surface of the parking area. He didn't ask if Jenna needed help.

He took her hand as she climbed on the seat and then made the big step out. Buddy followed, his feathery tail striking Abe's shoulder. Abe handed Pal to her, and she grasped both dogs' leashes, giving them room to sniff around.

After he finished securing the boat, Abe joined them. He motioned past a pale yellow house perched on a corner between the river and the road. Lights were blazing from it, which would make it more difficult to see the fireworks.

"There's an open field about a quarter of a mile to the west along this road," he said, switching on a flashlight.

Jenna walked between him and Buddy along the narrow road that was edged by small homes and cornfields where the stalks reached almost to her waist. He prayed his plan would work and his efforts wouldn't make it worse for her and Buddy.

"Don't be so nervous," she told him.

"Can you read my mind?"

"No, only your face. It displays your thoughts."

"I didn't realize that."

"I know." She smiled. "I wasn't going to tell you."

"Because you like knowing what I'm thinking."

"It saves time in the long run."

He laughed, the sound muffling the peepers and the frogs among the lily pads edging the river. Bending to get Pal who was rushing from one side of the road to the other, he picked her up and held her over one arm as they continued toward a square church.

It was a small, brick building, sitting at the edge of a field that was dotted with gravestones. Though there was a larger single-story brick meeting center at the other side of the parking lot, the church seemed as alone as when it'd been built almost three hundred years before. Or had there been a settlement close to the church? The parishioners wouldn't have lived far from where they worshipped.

Jenna took the flashlight from him and aimed it at the sign

beside the road. "The church is the *Rehoboth* church, but the town is spelled *R-e-h-o-b-e-t-h*. How did that happen?"

"The explanation I've heard is that the town used to be Rehoboth, but it got changed on a map, and it's been that way ever since." He led the way through the cemetery and around the trees ahead of them.

On the riverbank, away from any lights except fireflies, Abe switched off his flashlight. He laced his fingers among hers, keeping her close. When she gave his hand a gentle squeeze at the same moment the first fireworks blossomed in the sky, he wondered if he'd ever understood what happiness was before this moment.

She tensed beside him, and Buddy gave a low whine.

"Wait for it," Abe said. A very distant rumble was no louder than the sound his stomach made after a big meal. "We're almost ten miles from where the fireworks are being set off. Is this far enough?"

She nodded, then squatted to check on her dog. Buddy nuzzled her, and she pulled a treat for him and a smaller one for Pal from her pocket.

"He's okay?" asked Abe.

"More than okay." She stood.

He was about to ask another question, then realized she was watching the fireworks, enjoying them as she couldn't have on the farm. He stood beside her, more aware of her cheek close to him than the pyrotechnics in the sky. When the grand finale burst through the night, he cheered and clapped along with her.

"Thank you, Abe." The colors from the distant fireworks were dimmed by Jenna's smile. "Your kindness to Buddy and to me is… How do you say it? *Wunderbaar?*"

He chuckled. "We've got to work on your accent, but you're close. You'll learn more the longer you stay here."

"I'm not staying here, Abe." She pulled back a half step

and then another as if she was already leaving. "I thought you knew that."

"Where are you planning to go?" he managed to choke out. What a fool he'd been to think she might change her mind.

"Back home to Philadelphia. That's why I've been training with Buddy on search and rescue. I've got to try again to convince my boss to let us work as a team." She squared her shoulders. "I've got some new ideas he has to consider."

He didn't know how to answer. How could he ask her to stay and leave the life she loved? He ached in places he didn't know could ache as he thought of never seeing her again or hearing her sweet laugh. Was this how she'd felt the night she'd told him that she loved him and he'd thought she was making a joke? If so, he wondered how she could have ever forgiven him.

Jenna tried to act as if nothing was wrong while she rode in Abe's boat upriver to the landing behind *Grossmammi* Dinah's house. Getting out, she unhooked Buddy's leash, but carried Pal. The puppy had overtaxed herself and was limp with exhaustion.

While Abe tied up the boat, the dogs ran toward the house, Pal's fatigue forgotten. Moments later, a bone-chilling howl came from beyond the house.

Once, Jenna would have matched Abe's speed as he ran toward the sound. She stared in shock when she stepped around the side of the house and saw Buddy nudging Abe toward her truck. What was going on?

She got her answer when she saw something sticking out of her front tire. It looked like a chisel. When Abe reached out toward it, she shoved his hand aside.

"Don't touch it. There may be fingerprints on it."

"Mine." His voice was grim as he pulled out his flashlight and sprayed its beam along her truck. Gaping holes were in all four tires. "That chisel looks like the one from the tool chest in the barn. I used it a few weeks ago to carve out a new set of hinges for the door to the dairy tank room."

"Who else besides you knows the tools are there?"

"They're right out in the open, so anyone who goes into the barn could have seen them."

"Like my cousins?"

He whirled to face her. "Are you accusing Daryl and Geneva?"

She waved aside his question as Buddy came to stand beside her, his body tense. "No. I'm not accusing anyone." *I don't want your fingerprints to be the only ones on the handle.* She knew she could give him an alibi, but also knew that the authorities would have to question him. She took a deep breath. "I'm calling the police." She held up her hand when he opened his mouth. "Don't tell me because *Grossmammi* Dinah was Amish I should avoid getting the police involved."

"I wasn't. I was going to give you the chief's number."

"*You've* got the phone number for the chief of police?"

"*Ja.* There were some break-ins at the shop last year, and Art, our police chief, gave us his direct number so he could get there before any evidence was compromised. It helped discover who was behind the damage."

She nodded, took out her phone and made the call.

It was almost fifteen minutes later by the time a dark SUV pulled into the drive. When it stopped, she saw the words "Sweetwater Police" illuminated by the light from the porch. She walked out to meet the officer. Abe trailed her.

Jenna recognized, in the light from his car, the insignia on his uniform and nodded when Abe introduced her to Chief Damero. The chief of police was thin and below average height, but she could sense the coiled power within his slight form. His brown eyes displayed keen interest in everything and everyone around him, a trait skilled police officers had to hone. His white shirt and black trousers looked as if they'd just come off a hanger. He removed his broad-brimmed hat, setting it in his vehicle.

"Good to meet you, K-9 Sergeant Shetler," he said.

"And you, Chief."

Without another word, he motioned for Jenna to keep her partner calm and away from the truck. Her respect for the chief escalated. He must have worked with a K-9 before and knew Buddy would heed her orders.

Chief Damero listened as Jenna gave the same concise report she would have shared with her own supervisor. He took a few notes and then walked around the truck, checking it from every angle. Bending, he looked under the bed.

"They even slashed the spare." He straightened. "Whoever did it wanted to make sure you didn't go anywhere."

"Or they wanted to make a statement." She folded her arms.

"Have you made any enemies since you got here…" He checked his notes. "Since you got here last month?"

"None that I know of."

"Then you should think about some you don't know about."

She stepped aside as he pulled out plastic gloves and removed the chisel. He placed it in a plastic bag and labeled it.

"Art, you'll find my prints on that," Abe said quietly. "I used it recently."

"Thanks for letting me know." The police chief set the bag into a box in his vehicle. "I doubt we'll get any clear prints. Kids know to wear gloves to cover their trail." He ran his finger down his notes. "I've got everything I need for now. Come in tomorrow after ten, and I'll take your written statements. You know the drill, Sergeant. For now, I should get back." His mouth twisted in a grin. "Paperwork, you know."

"I do." She gave him a sympathetic smile and shook his hand again before he turned to reach for the driver's door on the SUV.

As the vehicle started to back out of the drive, Abe said, "He's a *gut* guy. If anyone can find out who damaged your tires, it'll be him. Art Damero— Wait a minute!" He grabbed her elbow. "Give me Dinah's latest letter."

She dug it out of her back pocket, unfolded it and handed it to him.

"Look." He pointed the flashlight at it. "See? The word 'Art' is capitalized."

"I know. I wrote the letter A with the others at the bottom."

"What if you're supposed to use the whole word?"

"Then it's Art Damero." She hobbled at her top speed toward the SUV, waving her arms over her head. "Chief! Wait a minute!"

The SUV squealed to a stop. Rushing to it, Jenna showed the chief the letter. She didn't have to explain what it was because he'd heard about her grandmother's odd will.

"Clocks are mentioned a lot." She gave him the letter. "Do you like clocks?"

"I don't think about them one way or the other." Chief Damero read the letter, then gave it back to her. "I mean, they're a tool."

Jenna faltered, but asked him to come inside. Abe followed as she'd assumed he would. She led the way upstairs to her grandmother's bedroom. She went to the mantel and took down a graceful walnut clock.

"My grandfather gave this to my grandmother the Christmas before they were married. It has to have been one of her most precious possessions."

"That clock isn't running," Abe argued. "The letter mentions ticktock, and even if this clock was running, you wouldn't hear it from the front porch."

"You're right. She must mean a clock downstairs, but which one?"

"Let's try the dining room first. Its windows open onto the screened porch."

Abe led the way and pointed out three clocks by the stack of quilts. "It could be one of these."

"I think she might have meant that one." Chief Damero walked over to the cuckoo clock that was half-hidden behind the china cabinet. "I didn't think Dinah would remember me in her will."

"You aren't the first to say that." Jenna smiled. "Everyone has been surprised what *Grossmammi* Dinah chose for them. Why do you think she wanted you to have an old cuckoo clock?"

"It's not a cuckoo clock." The chief took it off the wall, and Jenna realized her mistake when she saw a carved wooden fish leaping on its front. He explained the curving line behind the fish depicted the Pocomoke River. "I told her when I was young how much I wanted to catch a bass just like that one." His voice was thick with emotion as he pulled a black handkerchief from his pocket and dabbed at his eyes. "Dinah let me fish off her old pier and always consoled me about the big one that got away. It was amazing how her cookies and sweet tea always made me feel better."

"Enjoy it, knowing she knew how important it was to you."

The chief tried to speak, but was too choked. He nodded before carrying the clock as if it were as fragile as a milkweed blossom out to his SUV.

This time when he drove off, Jenna sat on the porch. Pal was asleep, curled against Buddy who was snoring. The sound of her partner's steady breathing was a gift she never would take for granted again.

Abe cleared his throat, then sat on the other rocker.

"Thanks for your help with the letter." Jenna stared straight ahead. "I don't know if I would have figured it out."

"You would have."

"Four letters down and two to go." She started to add more,

then turned away as the truth hit her. In two weeks, the last of the letters would have arrived, the last of the clues would have been followed and she could leave Sweetwater.

An uncertain future and a heart that wanted to tie her to the past urged her to reconsider. How could she? The farm was going to be inherited by someone, and she wouldn't have any excuse to return to Sweetwater.

Ever.

Chapter Twelve

In the two days since the fireworks, Abe hadn't spoken often with Jenna. She was always coming when he was going and vice versa. She needed to get her truck repaired, and that, along with training Buddy, demanded a lot of her time. Yet, he couldn't help feeling she was avoiding him.

He wanted to give her space, but he couldn't any longer. Tonight was the youth group gathering, and he needed her help in doing as the bishop had asked. The teens planned to get together around seven, so he arrived at Dinah's farm shortly after six.

He'd been shocked yesterday when Jenna had agreed to his plan for her to join the youth at tonight's meeting. She still had her reservations, but she'd listened to his plan and had reluctantly said she'd try it.

Her uncertainty had infected him. She was the professional, used to dealing with criminals. He had only his hopes that he could succeed at the task the bishop and God had given him.

He crossed the yard from the barn and peered around Dinah's back door. "Anyone home?"

He heard a faint answer before two dogs ran toward him, wagging their tails. Even so, he waited until Jenna came into the kitchen.

She opened the door and took the paper bag he held out. "What's this?"

"Some plain clothing. Sara Beth said these should fit you."

She looked in it. "I've got dark socks and black sneakers. I hope the dress is long enough to cover my prosthesis."

"It should be."

"If not, I'll let the hem down."

"Your hair—"

Her smile returned, lighting the room and the recesses of his heart. "No worries, Abe. I found a wig at a thrift store yesterday. It's set to go once I pin the *kapp* on to it. Give me a few minutes. I've got to force my hair under a wig, and that won't be quick."

Abe didn't answer before she hurried away. Her smile had undone him, forcing him to see the truth. He was miserable when she wasn't around, and he was happiest when she was nearby. It'd been that way when they were kids, but he had accepted her visits and leave-takings as part of the normal rhythm of the seasons. He'd come to think of fall as a dreary time and spring as filled with anticipation. Now he wondered if that had been because of Jenna's arrival each summer.

Sooner than he'd expected, he heard her on the stairs. She appeared in the kitchen, and he stared. He couldn't help himself. Not once had he imagined Jenna dressed in plain clothing or as a brunette. With a pair of heavy-rimmed black glasses large enough to conceal most of her freckles and the hem of the dark purple dress reaching the top of her sneakers, she could have walked past him on the street, and he wouldn't have recognized her. Then he looked closer. The twinkle in her eyes hadn't changed. Her smile as it slid across her lips still sent a tidal wave of warmth through him.

She turned in front of him. "What do you think?"

His breath caught as he viewed her from every angle. *Ja*, she was pretty, but it was her feisty spirit that made everything she did so vivid.

"What do *you* think?" he asked, trying not to reveal how he was fighting his craving to kiss her smiling lips.

"I feel ridiculous." She became serious. "Nobody is going to believe I'm an Amish teen from another district."

"They've just got to accept it long enough for you to get a feel for the group. After that, you can slip away if you want. I'll make sure you've got a way home. Trust me. Most of these kids are too interested in each other to pay attention to anyone else." He said that with confidence because, at the moment, a marching band could have paraded through the kitchen, and he wouldn't have noticed. His thoughts were solely of her.

"You're asking a lot."

"*Ja*, I've been praying a lot and asking God to help us reach the kids who are flirting with trouble."

"I hope He'll listen to you. He doesn't seem to listen to me."

"He's listening, Jenna. Sometimes the answer isn't what we want to hear."

She slipped the strap of the black handbag Sara Beth had included with the clothes over her shoulder. "I know you believe that."

Sorrow swept away other emotions. *God, please let Jenna know You love her. Touch her heart and bring it healing so she can listen for Your voice.*

Jenna said something, then turned to leave. He hadn't caught her words, and he didn't ask her to repeat them. Her face was blank, and he knew she was working to control her feelings. He hoped she'd succeed in corralling them tonight...and that he could, too.

Walking into the barn, Jenna hesitated, looking as if she were a new member of the running-around group of at risk kids. Her ears were poised to listen, and she was relieved to hear many of the conversations were in English. It was, she realized, because many of the topics revolved around modern gadgets. Words for those weren't available in *Deitsch*.

Some teens glanced in her direction, then away. She released the breath she'd been holding. If they'd recognized her, they would have stared and asked why a Philadelphia cop was infiltrating a get-together for plain teens. Getting herself a cup of the fruit punch from the middle of an otherwise empty table, she used it as a mask to conceal the lower half of her face. She noticed several women coming toward the table with trays topped with cookies and cake.

Ducking her head, Jenna turned away before Joyce Allgyer saw her face. She hadn't thought about who would be chaperoning tonight. Why hadn't she asked Abe more questions?

She edged into the shadows by some hay bales when she saw Abe stiffen on the other side of the room. Following his gaze, she gasped. Two of Abe's brothers were walking into the barn. Benuel and Homer were sure to recognize her.

Striding across the room to intercept them, Abe said, "You should have let me know you'd be here. We could have driven over together."

His brothers froze except for their eyes, which exchanged a look she didn't have any trouble translating. They hadn't expected to see Abe, and they weren't happy he was there.

Benuel donned a grin. "When did you start attending youth group again?"

"Just here to help make sure there's enough food for you bottomless pits."

"Plenty of popcorn, I hope." Homer rubbed his stomach. "Someone said there was going to be popcorn and lemonade tonight."

They went to the refreshments table. Behind them, Abe glanced at her.

Jenna didn't move from her spot, which gave her role as a shy newcomer credibility. From there, she could observe interactions among the plain teens who stood in groups, laughing and jostling and allowing some people to join in and closing their ranks on others. Nobody seemed to be offended. They bounced off one group like a ping-pong ball and became part of another. For the most part, the boys stayed with other boys while the girls stood elsewhere, talking and giggling and eyeing the boys who were keeping a close watch on them. It was the all-too-familiar teenage boy and girl interaction where everyone acted as if they weren't interested in anyone, even though they were.

Like her sister and Susan's friends had.

Susan had been the type of teen who'd belonged to a huge group that seemed to travel everywhere together. Members of the clique changed as some were invited in while others were squeezed out for some infraction, real or imagined. Susan had been the queen bee.

Jenna hadn't been jealous, just fascinated. She'd preferred her few close friends. At college, there had been three of them. The number never changed. Nor did the faces. They'd met at freshman orientation and stayed friends until…

Until the bomb exploded, and Jenna had let only Buddy in. She'd kept away her fellow cops who'd tried to break down the barriers, warning her in actions and words of the dangers of hiding within herself, of not reaching out to the community for the support they were eager to offer. She'd pushed everybody aside. Friends, family. Her blood relatives and her family that bled blue. They hadn't abandoned her; in fact, several had made superhuman efforts to reconnect with her. She'd ignored them, so consumed by anger and shame and loss she'd failed to realize they were offering her a way back to life. How many times had a fellow officer stopped by her hospital room or at rehab or even at her desk in the precinct and tried to start a conversation? She couldn't begin to count. Or maybe she didn't want to remember the many times she'd ended those conversations, envious of how their lives and duties hadn't changed.

Now here she was, sneaking around as she tried to stay invisible. Just as she had at the precinct. There, she'd been suffused by failure, and she hadn't wanted to face it or anyone in the department. At the same time, she'd been desperate to be accepted into the camaraderie she'd once taken for granted.

"Are you new?" asked a cheerful voice.

Jenna flinched, brought into the present by the simple question. She blinked twice hard and found herself looking at a girl who couldn't be much older than Sara Beth. The girl's hair was a medium brown and as curly as Jenna's was beneath the hot wig. A few lighter strands of the teen's hair had escaped to corkscrew by her eyes, and she pushed them toward her bun.

Jenna was glad the girl had spoken in English. "This is my first time here."

The girl glanced at the boys as they began to guffaw at a joke. "My name is Niva Stoltzfus. What's yours?"

"Sara Beth Glick," she answered, borrowing Abe's sister's name as well as Sass's.

Niva grinned and hooked a thumb over her shoulder. "Do you want to *komm* and meet the others?"

"*Ja.* In a minute." She lowered her voice. "Do you know where the bathroom is?" She looked at her empty cup. "I should have paced myself."

"*Komm mol.* I'll show you where it is."

Needing to contrive a way to discourage Niva's friendliness, Jenna was saved when a teen on the other side of the barn waved to Niva. "Just tell me where to go."

As soon as Niva explained which door to use in the farmhouse next to the barn, Jenna thanked the girl and edged toward the closest door. Looking over her shoulder as she walked out of the barn, she saw several kids watching her. Including Abe's brothers. Had they recognized her?

She went outside, pressing against the rough barnboards and grateful for the moonless night that left the yard in shadows. As she inched along the barn, she paused, holding her breath as she heard several boys talking. It wasn't easy to pick out their voices from the ones inside the barn, but she heard enough to realize they were discussing damage done to barns and chicken houses over recent months. She couldn't tell if they were bragging about their exploits or if they were as curious as the bishop about who was behind the crimes. Easing closer, she stopped when someone called to the boys, and they returned inside.

So close, but nothing!

A finger tapped on her shoulder, and she muffled her shriek. "Abe! Why are you trying to scare a year off my life?"

"Sorry." He separated from the other shadows. "Why are you out here?"

"Lots of reasons, but your brothers might have seen me and realized who I am. If they learn what we tried tonight, those kids won't trust you again." She didn't need to see his face to know he was disappointed.

It was obvious in his voice. "If you could go in for another few minutes—"

"No, Abe. I can't. I won't risk what's so important to you. Without me, you can focus on doing as you were asked. I don't want to be the reason you fail."

"I don't intend to fail."

"None of us do." As she spoke the words, she realized they were the truth. A truth she, in her arrogance, hadn't wanted to believe could be applied to her.

Only God doesn't make mistakes. Her grandmother's voice, chiding but comforting at the same time, rang through her head.

"There may be another way," she said. "Let me think about it, and we can talk about it more tomorrow."

"All right. You may be right."

She grasped his hands and gave them a quick squeeze. "Trust me. We'll find out what's going on and help these kids." She stepped away when a couple of teens walked out of the barn toward the house. "I should go."

"Do you remember how to drive a buggy?"

She nodded, hoping she was being honest.

"*Gut.* Take my buggy. I'll drive home with my brothers."

"They'll want to know why you aren't driving home yourself."

"I'll tell them the truth. I lent the buggy to a friend who needed it."

"It's always nice when you can cloak a falsehood in truth." She was pleased her words were teasing. She had to cover her disappointment at him calling her a friend.

When she'd arrived in Sweetwater a month ago, she'd been hopeful that they could resurrect their friendship. She should be thrilled his words confirmed they had. She wasn't. Her heart was begging to belong to him.

Yet she knew he was being smart.

So why was she being stupid?

Slowing her truck at the end of the drive two days later, Jenna pulled up to the mailbox and got out. She smiled as she heard Buddy's and Pal's eager welcomes from the house. Neither liked when she went somewhere without them. Knowing she would have to spend the next hour making it up to them, she smiled again. She loved every minute with the dogs.

She opened the mailbox and was shocked to discover a letter inside. Though she checked every day, she hadn't received anything but junk mail and flyers except on Tuesday.

It was Monday, and it still stung how useless her trip had been to the youth event. She hoped she'd have a chance to talk to Abe today about devising a way to uncover those behind the damaging pranks.

That would have to wait. Right now, there was a piece of first-class mail in the mailbox. Her eyes widened as she took it out. The letter was addressed to her. No return address, but the postmark was from Nevada. From her parents? Or junk mail designed to look like it was from someone she knew?

She opened the envelope and pulled out four pages. Words were scrawled across them as if someone had been writing in the middle of the night without a light on. As she began reading, nothing made sense. Then she realized the pages were out of sequence.

Shuffling them until they were in proper order, she was shocked. Why had her sister written after radio silence for so long? The scribbles and out-of-order pages didn't seem like Susan, who used a computer to print her correspondence on personalized stationery.

Jenna stuffed the pages into the envelope because the dogs' barking had risen to a frantic pitch. First things first. She opened the front door so the dogs could come out on the porch. They welcomed her as if she'd been gone for a year instead of two hours. She sat on the floor and let the puppy crawl over her. Buddy was a bit more dignified, but he stuck his nose into her ear. It was his way of showing he was willing to forgive her.

Fifteen minutes later, Buddy was stretched out beside her, his head balanced on her right leg while Pal fought sleep in her arms. She struggled to escape, but a low rumble from Buddy must have warned the puppy to stop. Within seconds, Pal was draped over Jenna's arm as if every bone in her body had turned to gelatin. Questions about why her sister had written to her in such a slapdash manner bothered her, but she focused on her best friend and the puppy.

Was Buddy her best friend? He was her partner, and she'd been so relieved in the hospital to hear he'd survived. Yet the words "best friend" brought a different image to mind.

Abe.

He'd been her best friend as a kid, but she wanted more now. For the past few days, she'd been having second thoughts about leaving Sweetwater after the last letter was delivered. Vic had made it clear there was no chance for her and Buddy to work together again. Her future—being stuck at a desk job. Perhaps it was time to reevaluate what she wanted to do. If only God would give her a hint what she should do, but He hadn't.

He's listening, Jenna. Sometimes the answer isn't what we want to hear.

"Enough already!" Arguing with herself wasn't getting her anywhere.

She pulled out the letter from her sister and opened it again. *Jenna*, the letter started.

Everything has gone wrong, and we need your help. Dustin bankrupted his company through stupid investments I warned him not to make, and—

Jenna sighed. Susan never let the chance pass to point out other's mistakes. "Don't be petty," she warned herself. Things must be horrific if her sister had contacted her.

—we're in danger of losing everything. There are so many liens against our house that, even if we sell it for what it's worth, we can't pay all of them off. The children hate going to school because their friends taunt them about Dustin's mistakes.

She translated that to mean other mothers were being less than kind to Susan—or Susan believed they were because she interpreted everyone else's behavior through the lens of how she would have acted if the situation was reversed.

As she read the rest of the letter, Jenna wondered how her

sister expected her to help. She had about five thousand dollars stashed away. Once Buddy had been retired from the police force, his medical and care expenses had become her responsibility. She hadn't hesitated, but his care had gutted her retirement fund.

We need a place to live where nobody knows about what happened to Dustin's company. You've always talked about how big your grandmother's house is, so we'll be joining you for the summer. Just the summer. I want to get the children into their own schools in the fall. I'll text our itinerary. Mom says you've got the same number.

The letter was signed "Susan." No *thank you*. No *love you*. Just Susan.

Jenna stared at the pages that bristled with desperation. Of course, she'd make room for her sister, Dustin and their two children as well as their French bulldogs, no matter how rudely her sister had assumed rather than asked. The last time Jenna had seen their kids, Harper hadn't been much more than a newborn and Liam a toddler. Now they were five and six. The bomb had stolen more than her leg. It had let her allow everything else to slide as she focused on rehab and trying to get her old job back.

The porch door opened, and Abe came in. Lines she hadn't noticed before were dug into his face. How worried was he that he'd be unable to do as the bishop had asked? Or was something else troubling him?

"Is that the letter from the lawyer already?" he asked.

Knowing he couldn't imagine any other reason why she'd be sitting on the porch looking bereft, she shook her head. "No. That won't come until tomorrow."

"I know it's not any of my business—"

"Stop it!" She surged to her feet. "Stop acting as if we're strangers."

Not giving him a chance to answer, she stormed into the house. The screen door slammed behind her. The sound created another barrage of pain that cut into her heart. She wasn't sure how many more blows it could take.

Closing his eyes so he didn't have to see the still vibrating door, Abe murmured a quick prayer. He needed God to help him choose the right words. He'd made a complete mess of this conversation, ending it before it'd begun. Jenna didn't usually slam doors. Not in anger. She was far more measured than that, but she was acting like his siblings when they were upset.

He opened the door and went into the house. *Is this the right thing, God? I can't let anger fester between us. That's happened before, and it hurt both of us.*

A chair scraped in the kitchen. Jenna was at the table with four pages spread out in front of her. She ignored him as he entered.

He put his straw hat on the table not far from the pages and sat beside her without waiting for an invitation. She continued to stare at the handwritten pages. The paper was a common white.

"Is it from your boss?" he asked. She hadn't said anything about talking to the police captain.

"No. From Susan. She wants to come here."

"Your sister wants to visit Sweetwater?" As far as he knew, Susan had never set foot on Dinah's farm.

"No, she wants to come here to live."

"Why?" The word exploded past his lips before he could halt it. *Get yourself under control.* Just because he was upset for Jenna was no excuse for asking such a prying question.

She gave him the gist. "They'll be here soon, but will they have a place to stay? There are two more letters coming. Tomorrow and next week. One of them has to explain what's going to happen with the farm. Then where will Susan and her family go? There's not enough room for them in my apartment in Philadelphia. It'll be a tight squeeze with Pal joining us." She blanched. "I don't mean that I consider the puppy more important than my sister and her family."

"I know. Do you believe Daryl would throw you out?"

"I do."

He sighed. "*Ja*, so do I. Have you considered you might end up with the farm?"

She shook her head. "*Grossmammi* Dinah told the Rickaboughs they'd get the farm. She wouldn't lie. Now my sister is coming here, and it's going to be a mess. I can't imagine Susan, Dustin or the kids here. They're city people."

"What about you? You live in Philadelphia." Why was he arguing? To keep himself from pulling her into his arms while he told her that whatever she faced, he wanted to face it with her?

"I spent summers here. I love the feel of freshly turned earth under my feet and mud between my toes. I don't know if Susan has ever gone barefoot. She wears flip-flops by the pool." Her face fell. "What am I going to do, Abe? How can I finish *Grossmammi* Dinah's bequests when I've got to take care of my sister, her husband and two small children? If I don't welcome them here, what are they going to do? *Grossmammi* Dinah would know what to do. I don't!"

Before he could answer, she leaned against his shoulder while sobs tore from her. Her tears soaked his shirt, and she gripped the front as if she feared being torn in two by her grief. Not just at being unable to see an easy way to help her sister, but for her doubts that she could complete the tasks Dinah had given her. The fear of failing her *grossmammi* was eating her alive. It was even more than that. The most important person in her life, the one who'd always been there for her during her childhood, was gone.

How could he have been so thoughtless?

"I'll be here for you," he whispered into her hair before he kissed the top of her head. He couldn't tell if she heard him or felt his lips. It didn't matter. He knew what he'd said and so did God. It was time to stop worrying about what would happen when she went away and think about what he could do while she was in Sweetwater. It might be the final thing he could do, before she left, to ease the pain in her heart.

Chapter Thirteen

Jenna overslept the next morning, so she was coming down the stairs to make coffee and let the dogs out for their morning romp when Abe came into the sunny kitchen with the mail. Unsure what to say to him after her tempest of tears yesterday, she took it without comment. She tossed the junk mail on the table, took a single glance at the letter and then asked Abe if he wanted any coffee.

Not waiting for his answer, she started preparing a pot. She needed a jolt of caffeine before she faced whatever the letter revealed. A glance at the clock told her that Daryl and Geneva should be appearing for their weekly update in less than an hour. She must have her brain working by the time they arrived.

Abe got milk from the fridge as she poured coffee for them and set the cups on the table before sitting. He sat as well but this time facing her instead of beside her. Was he trying to avoid a repeat of yesterday's sobfest? She wanted to assure him it wouldn't happen again. If she hadn't been so knocked off her feet by Susan's letter, she could have kept her emotions under control.

"Ready?" she asked.

He nodded. Was he as reluctant as she was to say any more than necessary?

"Let's see what my grandmother has to say this week."

"*Ja.*"

Hearing the tension in that single word, she reminded herself how his future was dependent on her cousins inheriting the farm. Her own future was hanging by a thread, so she understood his anxiety. She picked up the letter with the law office's logo on it, opened it and began to read it aloud.

"My dear *kins-kind*,

"Did you have fun solving my last letter? I remember how you loved word games when you visited me each summer. You'd wait for the newspaper to be delivered. First, you'd read the comics, and then if the weather was too hot or it was raining, you'd turn your attention to the crossword. Only when you had it filled in—or mostly filled—would you turn to the first page and start reading the news. On nice days, you'd leave the news until after supper. You were proud when, after you started to learn to read, we sat on the front porch and you'd read me the headlines. Within a year or two, you were reading the whole article out loud. You even read me recipes you thought sounded *gut* and hoped I'd prepare. Not that I ever could convince you to let me help you make those dishes. You weren't interested in learning to cook because you were too busy with the other *kinder*, which is how it should have been on lazy summer days.

"This letter is simple. You'll guess these answers if you think of what I've always told you were the three most important things in our lives. You need to start at the beginning and then go to the next and the next."

"Faith, family and friends," Jenna murmured.

One year, *Grossmammi* Dinah had made a stack of crib quilts that she'd donated to the local fire department for their annual auction. Each one had been a different color, but the words "Faith," "Family" and "Friends" had been appliquéd on top. Her grandmother had stated it was to give each *boppli* his or her first lesson in what was essential in life.

"I think you're right." Abe took the page and reread it. "Faith and family and friends. You're the only family she had left."

"There's Daryl and Geneva, and she considered Mom, my stepfather and Susan a part of her extended family."

He folded his arms on the table. "I should have known it wouldn't be that easy. What else does it have to say?"

> "Look high and low. Look up and down. Look over and under. Take note of what you see and heed what you find. Have fun, Jenna. We have one last game to play after this, so enjoy this one."

The tears threatened to overwhelm her again. It was the first time *Grossmammi* Dinah had mentioned an end to their communication, and Jenna knew it was the beginning of her farewell. She wasn't ready to let her grandmother go, along with this house. She would always have her memories, but it wouldn't be the same. While the letters had arrived each week, it had seemed as if her grandmother was still alive and would appear at any minute.

She raised her eyes to the saying displayed above the refrigerator. "'Behold, how good and how pleasant it is for brethren to dwell together in unity!'"

"Psalm 133," he said. "One of Dinah's favorites."

Standing, she peered at it. "There's one corner loose on the decal."

"Let me stick it back into place." He reached over her head and pressed on the corner. "It doesn't want to stick. Maybe something got on it. I can wipe it off."

She dampened a paper towel and handed it to him before opening the door to let Buddy and Pal in.

Abe gave a long, low whistle. "There's something stuck on here." He peeled it off and handed a slip of paper to her.

"'First cupboard, top shelf, back,'" she read. "Which cabinet is the first one? The one closest to the back door? The one beside that corner of the decal?"

"Dinah's clues have been literal. Is one cabinet older than the others?"

Jenna walked to a freestanding pine cupboard. "*Grossmammi* Dinah told me this was a wedding gift from her grandmother who had received it as a new bride from a great-uncle who had no children and wanted it to stay in the family because his mother had received it from her grandmother."

"That's at least six or seven generations."

Opening the door, she looked at the top shelf. She saw a bottle of mustard and an unopened jar of mayonnaise. She ran her hand along the shelf and paused when her fingers found a small wooden box. Lifting it out, she saw its top was decorated with a heart. At the center was carved "Psalm 127:3-5."

She pulled out her phone and did a quick search. "That psalm is 'Lo, children are an heritage of the Lord: and the fruit of the womb is his reward. As arrows are in the hand of a mighty man; so are children of the youth. Happy is the man that hath his quiver full of them.'" Shoving her phone in her pocket, she turned over the box. "Look, Abe!"

His eyes widened as he stared at the two names written on a piece of paper taped to the bottom. "Ezekiel and Barbara. My *daed*'s and *mamm*'s names."

She pressed the box into his hand. "*Grossmammi* Dinah wanted this to go to them. It's a message to be grateful for the children in their lives."

"They are grateful."

"You know she meant it to say more than that. She was always concerned how heavy your burden was, Abe, with you taking on the roles of father and mother along with big brother."

"I know."

She was amazed he'd admitted something he wouldn't have considered sharing when they were teens. "The message may be for you as well."

"If so, it's too late. Most of my siblings are grown."

"Except for Flossie and the twins." She put her hand on the small box. "*Grossmammi* Dinah wants you to give them a chance to know their parents."

"Easier said than done."

She shrugged her shoulders. "If you want to give up…"

Wagging a finger, he smiled. "I see what you're doing, Jenna. That's not the way to motivate someone. You should know dogs aren't the only ones who want a treat for a job well done."

"A treat? Like an extra cookie?"

He set the box on the table and clasped her shoulders. He tilted her toward him. "No, something sweeter. Like this."

His lips slanted across hers as she drew in her next breath. It was swept away by the heat that coursed across her mouth. The kitchen vanished, and they were back to the night when she'd dreamed he would kiss her just like this after telling her he loved her, too. The dream that had been shattered was mended and glorious.

As she slid her hands up his strong back, he drew her against the hard wall of his chest. The memory of every other kiss she'd shared was seared away, and there was nothing but this kiss, this man, this moment.

He continued to hold her close as he raised his mouth from hers. When she straightened his glasses, which had been knocked awry, he gave her a boyish grin that sent joy dancing through her heart.

Yipping came from around their feet as Pal gazed at them. Buddy had an open-mouthed grin, giving his approval.

She looked at Abe, and he gave her another smile as his mouth lowered toward hers.

The front door crashed into the wall. It'd already been open.

"The Rickaboughs," she whispered as she stepped away from Abe.

He caught her hand and pressed it to his lips, then released it as Daryl and Geneva strode in.

"Well?" asked Daryl, frowning at the dogs.

Pal backed behind Buddy who stood his ground and growled a low warning. When Jenna hushed him, her partner gave her a hurtful look before leading the puppy to a distant corner.

"No mention of the farm again this week." Jenna didn't bother to explain anything else. Daryl and his wife wouldn't care.

"I've had about as much of this as I can stand." Geneva's voice was shrill. "Someone needs to get me answers. Now!" Pointing at Jenna, she shrieked with frustration. "How much longer can this go on?"

Abe stepped forward. In their rush and blinding anger, it seemed that neither of the Rickaboughs had noticed him. A shame, because he could have held on to Jenna a while longer if he'd known they wouldn't see him.

The thought of her, as soft in his arms as he'd imagined, allowed him to answer with quiet dignity. "One week."

"How do you know?" snarled Daryl.

"Because there's one more letter, and it's coming next week, and it should have the answers we need."

Daryl swore and slammed his fist on the kitchen table, making it wobble. Abe wondered why the Rickaboughs were so desperate. It couldn't be money. They always seemed to have plenty to fix their house and buy new trucks.

Geneva sniffed and stamped out of the kitchen. Daryl followed, still cursing.

Abe paused, wanting to stay and pull Jenna to him again, but he said, "Let me try to calm Daryl."

"All right." She pressed her palm to his cheek.

It took every ounce of his strength to leave, but he didn't want Daryl to take more of his frustration out on Jenna. She already suspected her cousin had done the damage to her truck. Abe didn't want to believe that, but fury had twisted the man's mouth.

Calling to Daryl, he saw a cloud of dust over the drive. Geneva must have driven away already. Though he was curious why they'd brought two different vehicles, he was relieved to speak to Daryl without Geneva's drama.

"We need to talk about our agreement on the farm." Abe tried to ease into the point he wanted to make.

"Have you changed your mind?" Daryl's face turned a sickish shade of green. "We don't have the cash on hand to pay you for the work you've done."

"No, that's not what I mean. I'd still like to buy the farm."

"Glad to hear that." Daryl pulled a water bottle from the truck.

"It's frustrating to have to wait."

"Don't I know it!" He opened his water bottle and took a deep swig. "Sorry. Dust in my throat."

"Chickens make a lot of dust, ain't so?"

Daryl screwed the top on the bottle. "I should have known that batty old lady would mess up everything. We should contest the will."

"That would take even longer and could mean the farm is divvied up between you and Jenna. Neither of you want that."

"No. She wants to get back to the city, and I want to get on with my life." His smile didn't have a hint of warmth. "Just like you do."

Abe let his shoulders ease from the tension that wrapped heavy chains around them. "So our agreement is still *gut*?"

"As good as it ever was." He clapped Abe on the arm. "Let's go to the diner. You can buy me a cup of coffee, and I've got ideas for things you can do while the estate goes through probate. What do you say?"

I want to kiss Jenna again. He couldn't say that for a lot of reasons. It was important to remain on Daryl's better side for now. Jenna would understand, ain't so? He didn't listen to his conscience warning him he was making a big mistake. Instead, he got into the truck and didn't look back.

Jenna's phone rang when she was on her stomach by the sofa. *Grossmammi* Dinah hadn't been fooling when she wrote Jenna needed to look high and low. The search might have gone more smoothly if Jenna could keep her mind on her task instead of replaying each moment of Abe's kisses.

Groping for her phone and shoving Buddy's inquisitive nose away from her face, she answered as she would have at the precinct. "Shetler here."

She heard Chief Damero's gruff hello, and she pushed herself up. "What can I do for you, Chief?"

"I'd appreciate it if you'd stop by in about an hour."

"Is this about my slashed tires?'

"We'll talk when you get here."

"Okay."

He grunted an acknowledgment and hung up. She stretched her arm under the sofa again, trying to find the item her fingers had brushed. There! Curving her hand around it, she dragged it out. A cardboard box about the same size as the one Sass had used to store the old quilt.

Pal and Buddy nosed around it, then walked away while she got up and put it on the sofa.

"Oh, my!" she gasped when she saw Susan's name printed on the paper taped to the top.

Inside were two black purses. Their style was from the '50s. Susan had been obsessed with vintage since she and Dustin had bought their first home, a midcentury bungalow near the Las Vegas Strip. Beneath the purses were scarves and mittens knitted in *Grossmammi* Dinah's bright yarn. More than two dozen pairs in a variety of sizes.

"I never guessed that you made a set for me to take to Susan," Jenna whispered, "and another set in case she came here." Again she was awed by her grandmother's huge heart, though Susan had wanted nothing to do with "your backwater granny."

At the very bottom of the box was a pillow. "The mercy of the Lord is from everlasting to everlasting upon them that fear Him, and His righteousness unto children's children" was embroidered on one side in mint green. On the reverse was: "Psalm 103:17."

Replacing everything in the box, Jenna ran her hands over the knobbly mittens. She thought of her grandmother's hands. They'd been as lumpy and uneven from years of hard work. Blinking back tears, she closed the box. Susan would arrive soon. Would she finally appreciate what *Grossmammi* Dinah had done for her?

Jenna tried to imagine Susan at the farm. She couldn't. Besides, it was nicer to revel in the memory of Abe's kiss. She hadn't seen that coming. What would happen now? She had no idea, but she couldn't wait to find out.

Art Damero's office appeared to be lost in the aftermath of a paper tornado. Jenna wondered how he found his desk, then guessed he used one of the empty ones in the bullpen.

The chief strode in. He motioned toward a sofa beside the left-hand wall, then grabbed a stack of manuals and set them on others stacked on a filing cabinet. "Coffee?"

"If it's fresh." She sat.

He grinned. "Spoken like an experienced cop. The only thing worse than no coffee is—"

"Yesterday's coffee."

"Let me check." He walked out and returned with two steaming cups. "Just finished dripping."

"Perfect." She balanced the cup on the sofa's arm. Waiting while the chief talked about the weather, about fishing and the crabs he was going to enjoy that weekend, she hoped he wasn't delaying because he had something bad to tell her.

After nearly fifteen minutes, he cleared his throat. "Are you planning to stay in Sweetwater?"

"I haven't made any plans for after I'm done with my grandmother's will."

"We've got an open slot for a cop here." He looked at his empty cup. "I talked to your supervisor in Philly, and he had nothing but good things to say about you and your partner. Said you could be an asset here."

She forced her smile to remain in place. Trust Vic to give her a great recommendation so he could replace her. "That was nice of him."

Chief Damero gave her a knowing grin. "He was piling the compliments on extra hard. Got me wondering why. Are you a problem he wants to get rid of, or is he fool enough to think he could confuse this hayseed cop with fancy city talk?"

She laughed. There wasn't anything hayseed about Chief Damero. He was quick-witted and dedicated to his job.

"Vic thinks he's going to be the basis for the next big cop screenplay," she replied. "The one he's been writing for the past five years."

The chief roared with laughter. "Gotcha. I've met the type far too often. More interested in impressing his superiors than serving the public." He became serious again. "The offer is open, Jenna. We could use you here."

"I'll think about it," she replied. "Any news on who ruined my tires?"

"Nothing specific I can share with you yet." Frustration, as deep as Daryl's, crept into his voice. "You've heard we've had a lot of trouble around here with teens. They're smart and elusive. I'd love to catch them in action, but I don't have the manpower to watch the whole area."

Jenna nodded, but her mind was whirling with an idea. Thanking the chief for his offer, she hurried back to the farm, eager to refine the inspiration with Abe.

As she'd hoped, Abe was milking. Watching him pat the cow and speak to her as if she comprehended everything he said, Jenna walked along the narrow area between the two rows of cows.

When he noticed her, he gave her a bone-melting smile. She forced her mind to remain on what she'd come to tell him instead of kissing him again.

"I was talking with Art Damero," she said, "and I got an idea."

He poured the milk into the can and motioned for her to follow him toward the tank where he stored it. "Does he know who slashed your tires?"

"Not yet." She waited for him to turn so she had his full attention. "I want you to spread the word the dogs and I won't be here this weekend. That might draw out the vandals."

"You're setting a trap." He set the pails on the floor.

"Every incident other than my tires has been on a Friday night. Maybe if we make this place look empty, they'll bite."

"If they don't?"

"We don't lose anything but a night's sleep."

He frowned. "Did Art ask you to do this?"

"No. It's all my idea."

He walked to the cows, and she followed. "Are you going to tell him?"

"No. So will you help me spread the word I won't be here?"

"On one condition."

Surprised, she asked, "What?"

He bent to wash a cow's udder. "I'm with you when you set this trap Friday, and you don't bring your gun."

Jenna didn't want to agree. Abe guessed the damage was being done by plain kids, but if he was wrong, the situation could go sour. Fast. "All right. We'll start spreading the word around Sweetwater. Meanwhile, I'll work on details for our stakeout. I like having the j's dotted and x's crossed."

He chuckled and moved to take the other automatic milker off a cow. "Isn't it 'dotting the i's and crossing the t's?'"

"I don't like doing everything just like everyone else."

"I've noticed that. All right. I'm in. Friday night let's put an end to the vandals' spree."

Chapter Fourteen

Everything in the plan Jenna had devised with Abe threatened to fall apart Friday morning. The younger Bontranger *kinder* came down two days before with a virus that left them feverish and coughing, and Sara Beth didn't want to tend to them because she was afraid of catching it and endangering her possible baby. She still hadn't made an appointment with a doctor, and Jenna planned to call on Monday to arrange for Abe's sister to go in. Jenna would make sure Sara Beth went. Benuel and Homer refused to stay home because they'd made other plans with friends.

Then there was the issue of the dogs. If Buddy or Pal began to bark, the troublemakers would flee before the trap could be closed around them. Where could the dogs spend Friday night? Not at the Rickaboughs. She would have put an end to the stakeout before letting her cousins watch the dogs. Even if they'd been willing.

She turned to Mr. Carpenter, who was anxious to have her and Abe take a ride in his Model A as soon as he got it running. He was happy to have the recovering twins and the dogs spend the night with him. Though he had a couple of cats, they didn't even bother to hiss at the dogs when Jenna brought them over for a visit. The calico and the tiger had stretched in a way that said they were too important to be bothered by mere canines. When the cats had walked away,

Pal had tried to give chase, but Jenna kept her close until the puppy decided she'd rather spend time with the old man. The twins were eager to play with the toys Mr. Carpenter kept for his grandchildren's visits, and Jenna guessed they would persuade him to let them watch some television, something they couldn't have done at home.

Now the farm was dark, and it looked as deserted as it must have after *Grossmammi* Dinah's death. Low clouds hung over the horizon, adding to the humidity. Sweat trickled down Jenna's spine as she remained inside the barn, out of sight of the open door.

Next to her, Abe couldn't hide his anxiety. He stood, then he sat before standing again. He'd started to pace, but stopped when she warned him any motion could tip off anyone looking to do mischief. A single glance in his direction was enough to warn him not to keep tapping the toe of his boot on the concrete floor.

That had been two hours ago when they first slipped into the barn after Jenna made a big show of leaving with the dogs. Two hours of silence and wiping away sweat and trying to stay awake when her eyes were burning from trying to see through the night.

How could she have forgotten how much she hated doing a stakeout? When she'd been accepted into the training program to become a K-9 officer, she'd been so glad to put the boredom and either too cold or too hot nights behind her. Now, here she was, doused in bug repellant, and lurking in the corner of her grandmother's barn.

It had to work! She and Abe had spread the word through Sweetwater. She'd made a point of discussing her plans to spend the weekend in Ocean City, telling everyone she met in stores and along the street. She smiled at the suggestions of where to eat and what to see. She even mentioned that the dogs would be gone, too. Abe had assured her that he'd spent the past three days mentioning her plans among the Amish when teens were nearby.

She brushed away yet another mosquito. She couldn't re-apply the bug spray because its soft hiss might alert anyone nearby. Too many thoughts raced through her head and begged her to talk to Abe. She bit her lip to stay quiet.

Then she heard something. A footfall? Yes! Another! She grabbed Abe's arm to alert him at the same time he reached for her hand.

Jenna drew away as a delightful sensation rippled from his fingers to her brain. She had to focus.

She crept forward for a better view. She stuck close to the wall, moving a few inches, then pausing and listening. Two muffled voices. More footsteps. Her fingers dropped to where her pistol should be, then clenched. She hoped Abe was right about the pranksters being Amish.

She motioned for Abe to remain where he was as she went to the other door. Slipping out, she came around behind the trespassers. Her brows rose when she saw two forms huddled with small containers in their hands. In the dim moonlight, she could see they wore Amish men's clothing, but she didn't let herself assume anything. *Englisch* teens could be disguising themselves, ready to put the blame on plain kids.

Keeping to the shadows cast by the barn, she inched closer. They were speaking *Deitsch*. She couldn't understand what they were saying, but caught a few words she recognized. Nothing that revealed who squatted in front of her.

She took a deep breath and raised her chin, trying to look bigger.

Suddenly the kids stiffened. She'd been silent, but some-thing must have alerted them. They turned to bolt.

She ran forward, clasping her hands together as if she held a gun. "Stop right there! Police!" Though she didn't have a radio either, she called, "Captain, we've got them! Send in the rest of the team."

The two froze, clutching each other. Two containers fell from their hands and rolled across the grass. She didn't take her eyes off them as she stepped forward, one decisive step at a time. When she ordered them to drop to the ground and keep their hands over their heads and in her sight, they did.

Abe walked out of the barn. He didn't speak as he walked to the prostrate forms. She closed the distance between her and the boys, too, not wanting them to think they could try to overwhelm an unarmed man.

When he stood in front of them, Abe gasped. "Benuel! Homer!"

Abe stared at his younger brothers, wanting to deny what was right in front of his eyes. He couldn't. When the boys stood and hung their heads, he wasn't sure they were sorry they'd been about to damage Dinah's barn. He was sure they were sorry they'd gotten caught.

Just as he was heartsick that his brothers had been revealed as the vandals.

"What made you think of destroying others' property?" he asked.

Jenna strode forward from where she'd been picking up what he could see where aerosol paint cans. She shook them, and he could hear the rattle of the plastic balls inside them.

"Don't answer that," she said sharply.

"What?" Why was she telling his brothers that?

She cut her eyes to him for a second, keeping her attention on his brothers. "Anything they say now we could be asked to repeat in court." The sick feeling in his heart dropped into his gut as she handed him the paint cans and pulled out her cell phone. "I'm going to call Chief Damero. He'll read them their rights and take it from there."

"No."

She scowled. "What do you mean? He needs to take your brothers in for questioning. We'll need to make our statements, too."

"You can't call the police."

"Why not?"

He shook his head and lowered his voice so the boys couldn't overhear. "I told you Elden asked me to get involved so the authorities wouldn't have to."

"The authorities are already involved because *I'm* involved. Abe, you can't ask me to look the other way while the bishop gives these boys a slap on the wrist. They've been caught trying to commit a crime."

"It's not our way."

"But it's *my* way."

"You can't contact the police until Elden has seen the situation. What does another hour matter?" He gestured toward her phone. "Call him. He'll hear the phone in his shop."

"At this hour? It's got to be after midnight by now. How?" She glared at him. "You told him what we were planning ahead of time, didn't you?"

He didn't answer. Whatever he said now would make the situation worse.

Everything had changed.

Nothing had.

God, he prayed in despair, *why have You put a love for Jenna in my heart when we belong to two different worlds? I can't ask her to stop being what she is, and I can't walk away from what You expect me to be. Is there any path we can walk together, or is it hopeless?*

The bed bounced, and Jenna came awake between one breath and the next as two cool noses snuck under the sheet to press against her ear.

Opening her eyes, she smiled at eager canine faces. "What are you up to?"

She pushed Buddy and Pal away far enough so she could sit. They gave her droopy, disappointed faces, and she was about to laugh when she recalled why she'd slept so late this morning.

Abe had been adamant that plain kids must be dealt with by the Amish. She refused to let him take the paint containers with him when he led his brothers to the bishop's house. Then she'd called Chief Damero.

It hadn't been a comfortable conversation, because she hadn't named the almost graffiti bandits, explaining they were plain and he needed to speak with Elden. He didn't act surprised at the request, but she couldn't get past her feeling he was disappointed in her.

Why shouldn't he be? She was disappointed in herself for not insisting Abe listen to her. How her ex would crow with laughter that she hadn't pressed her point further! Richard had called her obstinate and too much in love with the rules. How could that be when Abe had teased her for liking to do things differently?

She was confused, caught in a maze of her own making with no idea how to escape. She tried while she made breakfast for herself and the dogs. She wondered if Abe had come to milk the cows, but couldn't bring herself to check. What could she say to him? That she believed he had made a huge mistake? He hadn't wanted to hear that last night; he wouldn't be any more open-minded today.

Even so, when she heard the door open, her heart stopped in midbeat, hoping against hope that it was Abe.

It wasn't. Sara Beth stood in the kitchen, fear making her face pale. "I haven't been honest with you."

"About what?"

"I've been to see a *doktor.*"

Her grin felt strange on her face, but it was sincere. "Sara Beth, I'm happy to hear that. What did the doctor say?"

"She ran a bunch of tests and told me to *komm* today to get the results." She raised her eyes to meet Jenna's gaze. "Will you go in with me? You're *Englisch*, and you know more about how *doktors* talk than I do."

Jenna tapped her prosthesis. "The one thing I learned from getting this is how important it is to have someone with you because it's easy to miss something the doctor says."

"So will you go with me?"

"Of course."

"*Danki.*" She gestured toward the door. "We need to go, or I'll be late."

"Your appointment is now? On a Saturday?"

"*Ja.* Why else would I have *komm* over to ask you to go with me?"

Pausing to make sure the dogs were fine, Jenna left with Sara Beth. She suggested they take her truck, and Sara Beth smiled for the first time. Jenna guessed the girl had never ridden in a pickup before.

Her smile vanished along with Jenna's when they saw Abe step around the side of the truck. Not even making an attempt to be polite, Jenna demanded, "What are you doing here?"

"I was working in the barn." His tone wasn't as cold as hers. "I saw Sara Beth, and I wanted to check on her."

"You don't have to worry," Jenna said. "I won't contaminate her."

"You know I don't think that."

"To be honest, I've got no idea what you think about anything. Now, if you'll excuse us, Sara Beth doesn't want to be late for her appointment."

Abe looked at his sister. "Where are you going?"

Sara Beth answered, "To the *doktor*'s."

"Do you want me to go with you?"

"No."

Abe's face fell, and Jenna saw how hurt he was. As Sara Beth climbed into the truck, Jenna wished she could think of something to say to ease Abe's pain.

She couldn't. Not without opening herself to more.

Abe drew in the reins of his buggy in front of Dinah's farm the following Thursday. It had been the worst week of his life. Sara Beth had shut him out, not telling him what had happened at the *doktor*'s office. Because he wasn't her *daed*, he couldn't go there—even if he'd known which one it was—and ask. His parents had been so busy with new orders, he didn't think they even noticed that Elden had visited every day to speak with Benuel and Homer.

Jenna had acted as if he didn't exist. If she happened to be outside when he was feeding the Highland cows or doing other work in the yard, she went in the house without acknowledging him. He'd thought about going in, but as he approached the house, he heard Buddy's unmistakable growl. The German shepherd was protecting his partner, and Abe would have been a fool to try to walk past him to confront Jenna. What could he say to her? He couldn't apologize for following the tenets of the Amish, and she wasn't willing to change either. They were stuck, drowning in sorrow.

Though he'd been itching to find out what Dinah's last letter had said, Jenna hadn't shared it. He couldn't believe she'd be so petty as to keep the future of the farm from him. He'd kept an eye out for her packed bags, but he saw no sign of her leaving. What had the letter said?

Abe pushed that thought away. He wasn't here to talk about the farm. He was here because nobody had seen Zeke and Zoe since breakfast, and it was time for supper. He jumped out of the buggy at the end of the drive as Jenna closed the mailbox and flipped the metal flag to alert the mail carrier a letter waited inside.

She was alone.

He glanced toward the house. Buddy was on the porch, sound asleep.

Alone.

Where was Pal? The puppy didn't go far from the German shepherd.

He'd been so certain the twins would be here. They loved to play with the dogs and the tire swing as well as help Jenna with training Buddy.

"You look upset, Abe," Jenna said. "What's wrong?"

"Have you seen the twins?"

"No." Her face tightened into what he'd come to think of as her "cop expression." Taut, emotionless, alert. "How long have they been missing?"

"Since breakfast."

Her mouth became a straight line. "This could be serious, Abe. You've got to contact the police."

"I am. I'm talking to you."

"Abe—"

"We can argue later. You've been training Buddy to find lost people. Can he find the twins?"

"We've only started his training."

He seized her hands, not wanting to let her walk away. "I need you and Buddy to help me find Zeke and Zoe."

"I don't know if Buddy can help."

"I don't either, and we won't know unless we let him try."

She met his gaze. So many emotions filled her eyes he wasn't sure which one she would go with. He prayed it was compassion.

"I'll help you as long as you agree I can alert the Sweetwater police. I know you want to be faithful to the life you've been raised in, but did you know your bishop is going to meet with Chief Damero about your brothers?"

"No. When?"

She waved aside his words as she pulled out her phone. A quick message was left with the 911 operator and then Jenna asked him, "I need something of Zoe's and something of Zeke's. A piece of clothing they've just worn and which hasn't been washed is the best."

"I don't have anything."

"Let me see if there's something in the house."

Abe followed her onto the porch. Buddy eyed him, but didn't move as they went into the house.

"Where's Pal?" Jenna looked at the rooms on either side of the hall, then hurried to the kitchen. "Her leash is gone."

"I'll give you one guess who took it and her."

She suddenly smiled. "That should make this easier. The kids have been over every inch of this yard. I don't know if Buddy can pick out newer scents among old ones. But I don't let Pal go near the road. If Buddy can pick up a trail there, we may be able to find them."

She took a blanket from the puppy's bed and carried it out to the porch. Calling to Buddy, she led the way to the road. There, she held the blanket out to Buddy. He sniffed it and wagged his tail.

"Got it?" she asked.

Buddy looked at her, his eyes glistening in anticipation of the playtime that would come when he succeeded. He didn't have any doubts about finding the puppy. Abe prayed Jenna didn't either because he was riddled with them himself. The twins hadn't wandered off like this before.

She raised her hand, then dropped it to her side. "Go. Find."

Abe watched as the dog nosed around the verge. Buddy barked and headed along the road.

She followed and threw over her shoulder, "What are you waiting for? Let's find Pal and the twins!"

Chapter Fifteen

Jenna panted as she kept up with Buddy. The early evening was thick with humidity, and thunder rumbled off in the distance. Storms had bypassed the area all week, but this one looked as if it had them in its sights.

Wishing she'd brought something to keep the beads of perspiration away from her eyes, she winced as a salty drop seared her right eye. It watered, but she didn't slow as Buddy led her and Abe along the road for almost a mile, then turned onto a dirt path running between two fields. On one side was corn. The other was planted with soybeans. She had no idea whose fields they were and was relieved when her partner didn't cut through the plants. The twins were old enough to avoid the sharp edges of the corn's leaves.

Behind her, Abe was keeping pace. He'd offered once to take the leash. She refused, not sure how Buddy would react to someone else holding it.

"We've gone in a circle," Abe said as they returned to the road that ran parallel to the river. "Has he lost the scent?"

She looked at Buddy who had his nose high in the air, drawing in every particle he could. He was keeping a steady pace.

"I don't think so." Her left leg throbbed more with every step.

"Call him to take a break."

"No. I'm okay."

He put his arm around her waist, helping her keep moving forward before the dog ran along a wood fence leading toward the river. At a half-opened gate, Buddy squeezed through and kept going.

Jenna let the leash play out as she edged through the gate. Abe climbed over the slats. The high grass tried to trip her, but she pushed toward the far side of the field where Buddy had paused, sniffing the air. His whole body was taut. He wasn't barking, so she knew he hadn't found Pal there.

Reeling in the leash, she reached her dog. He looked at her with an expression she deciphered as dismay.

"We need to find Pal. Find."

They went on, following the fence on this side of the field. When Buddy led the way to another gate, this one closed, Abe didn't hesitate. He unlatched the gate, let them through and then shut it again.

"We're on the Rickaboughs' land." Abe pointed to a trio of long, low barns. Beside them were what looked like small silos set on legs. "Those are their chicken houses and their feed storage."

"That can't be right." Jenna stared at the weatherworn barns with dark gaps along the sides. "Why would they leave the doors open? Won't the chickens escape?"

"*Ja*, they would." He took her hand as they walked with the dog toward the barns, which looked deserted. "What's going on here? If they had to destroy their flocks because of the bird flu, everyone would be talking about it."

She was about to answer when she heard a dog bark. "Is that Pal?"

"Could be."

Buddy began to lope toward the closest barn. She wondered how many apologies it would take to calm her cousins when they found out the puppy had gotten into their chicken house. Were the twins with her?

Then another dog barked and another and another until there was a chorus coming from the barn.

Jenna took a deep breath before she went inside, not wanting to breathe in the odors of the chickens. It burst out of her in shock when she realized she didn't have to worry about poultry of any kind.

The huge space was filled with wire cages, stacked two and three high. In each was at least one dog. The puppies of the smaller breeds, like spaniels and border collies, were crammed six or seven into a cage that had room for a single dog. They were the ones barking. The older dogs stared at them, fearful and resigned. Many had runny eyes and marks from healing wounds on their faces and bodies.

Buddy whined and leaned against Jenna, looking for comfort. She put her hand on his head as she tried to count the number of cages and the dogs. It was impossible because there were cages behind other cages. Droppings and other disgusting things covered the floor.

"A puppy mill," she breathed in horror. "Daryl is running a puppy mill."

Abe muttered something under his breath. Before she could ask what he'd said, a motion in the center of the aisle caught her eyes. A puppy that was trying to stick its nose into a cage with a bunch of other small dogs.

Buddy sat and barked.

It took her a second before she realized what he meant. Then she was rushing forward to the puppy. "Pal." She snuggled the puppy close to her, not caring how much Pal stank.

"Is she okay?" Abe patted the puppy as he scanned the barn, looking for his brother and sister. "Zeke! Zoe! Are you in—?"

A scream cut him off. Not from inside the barn. Outside.

Buddy took off like a furry bullet, nearly pulling Jenna to the ground. She called for him to halt, then shoved the puppy into Abe's arms and her phone into his hand.

"Call the cops!" she ordered.

She didn't wait for him to argue with her. Gripping Buddy's leash more tightly, she told him to track. She followed Buddy toward the house. He leaped up the back steps and pawed the back door. Stretching past him, she opened it. He leaped inside. She almost tripped over him when he stopped, barking. His hackles rose, and his lips curled in a snarl.

Another scream. A child!

Looking across the pristine kitchen, she saw a terrified Zoe. The child started toward her, but was jerked back so hard she fell to the floor. She began to cry, but Geneva ignored her as she stepped over the child.

"Get that filthy dog out of my house!" Geneva shouted as Abe came inside, still carrying the puppy.

"Buddy wouldn't be filthy if he hadn't been inside your puppy mill!" Jenna's clenched fingers, opening and closing like an Old West gunslinger waiting to go for his gun, should have warned Geneva she was furious. "We'll take the kids and my dogs and leave."

Daryl pushed into the kitchen, shoving Zeke ahead of him. The little boy helped his crying sister up. When he started for his big brother, Geneva held both kids. "Not so fast."

"Let them go." Jenna didn't dare to look at Abe. If she saw his fear for his siblings, she might lose her hold on her outward serenity. "We can talk about this. The children don't need to be involved."

"They already are." Daryl pulled a rifle out from behind a tall cabinet and set it on the table. It was a warning he was the one who could choose who survived and who didn't. Jenna had seen other punks try the same thing.

Please, God, let this end without anyone getting killed. How many times had she sent up that same prayer? How many times had it been answered? So many times that her faith should be as unyielding as Abe's. *I'm sorry I didn't see Your loving hand then.*

Daryl went on, "Your kids have been nosing around. Who knows what damage they've done to our dogs?"

Abe stepped forward, stopping when Jenna put a hand on his arm. His voice was stiff with anger. "You're not going to blame the wounds and sickness those poor animals are suffering on anyone else!"

"What are you going to do about it?" Geneva taunted. "Go ahead and call the authorities. We know how to deal with them. They're as easy to fool as you are, Abe Bontranger. You swallowed our bait—hook, line and sinker. Did you really think we'd sell you Dinah's farm? It's got to be worth twice what you offered for it."

"We had an agreement."

"Not a real one," Daryl sneered.

"Except our word." Abe clasped his fisted hands behind him. Jenna wasn't worried he'd try to strike her cousin. No matter how angry Abe was or how fearful for his little sister and brother, he wouldn't raise his hands against someone else.

Why had she failed to see conserving his plain ways required as much compromise from him when his emotions were high as her determination to retrain Buddy and return to work had proved to be for her? When she'd been a street cop, she'd learned the value of de-escalating a tense situation with calmness. Her last choice would be using a weapon. That, she realized with amazement, wasn't any different from what Abe was doing now.

Geneva wore a superior smile. "Now Jenna Rose needs to hand over the letter that says who gets the farm."

"I don't have it." Jenna's soft voice silenced the kitchen.

"You don't?" asked Abe, looking at her in astonishment. "It's Thursday. The letters come on Tuesday."

"Not this week. I didn't get the letter from the lawyer." She wanted to add she'd checked the mailbox hourly for the past two days, but it'd remained empty.

Geneva flicked her fingers toward the door. "Stop playing around. Go and get the letter like a good girl. You know better than to contact your police pals."

"Pal?" cried Zoe. "Don't hurt Pal!"

"Tell her to shut up," Daryl ordered at the same time his wife asked, "What's she talking about?"

Zeke frowned. "They hurt puppies. Lots of puppies like Pal, but sicker."

Clarity struck Jenna. "You've been shooting dogs after dark, haven't you? Why? Because they can't be bred any longer?"

"Putting them out of their misery." Daryl shrugged. "You wouldn't want them to suffer, would you?"

She shook her head in disgust and pointed to Pal, who cowered in fear next to Abe. "Did this puppy escape, or did you leave her on the road to die?"

"Don't answer that, Daryl." Geneva put her hand on the rifle on the table. "She's a cop. Everything you say can be used against you. Get the letter, Jenna Rose."

"I told you. There isn't a letter." Jenna kept her voice steady.

"There has to be a letter." Daryl put his hand on the table beside the gun. "Do you think we're stupid?"

"I think you're desperate," she replied so she didn't have to say they were witless…and cruel and greedy. "But threatening the twins or us isn't going to get you that information today."

Geneva glanced at her husband. "Maybe Ken—"

"He doesn't know what's in the letters," Jenna interrupted.

"He could open it."

Abe said, "If he has it. I'm sure he mailed it out days ago."

"If the letter has been lost in the mail, we'll never know who gets the farm." Daryl cradled his head and moaned.

"There may be something else. Dinah was *gut* with details.

Maybe she wrote it somewhere else after she told you she was leaving you her farm."

Daryl's face became a strange shade of grayish-green. "She didn't exactly tell us that."

Abe frowned. "Have you been lying right from the beginning? You thought you could get free labor out of me while you spent your time abusing dogs."

"Not my fault you believed us."

"Daryl, shut up!" His wife punched his shoulder.

He kept talking. "It was for nothing. Without a will, the farm will go to Jenna."

Geneva grasped the gun and raised it toward the twins, struggling to move the long gun in the cramped space. "Get a pen and paper, Daryl. Jenna will sign the farm over to us."

"I'll do that if you let the others go." Jenna riveted her gaze on her cousins. She knew the time to talk sense had come and gone.

The Rickaboughs exchanged another glance, this one ending with matching greedy smiles on their faces.

"Jenna, no," Abe said.

"Take the kids and the dogs and go. Now!" She waved to her cousins. "Get me something to write on."

Geneva kept the gun pointed at the Bontrangers as Abe gathered the twins and herded them toward the door.

"Buddy, out with Pal," she ordered.

The dog didn't want to obey, but he did, following Abe, the twins and the puppy out of the house.

Or so she thought until Abe came to stand beside her. The kids and the dogs were outside, running away from the house.

In a strangled whisper, she said, "Abe! What are you doing here?"

"I couldn't miss the ending."

"Ending?"

Police sirens ripped through the air from every side of the

house. A voice shouted for the Rickaboughs to come out with their hands up. The kids must have alerted them to what was happening in the house.

Geneva raised the gun, but Jenna grabbed the long barrel. She yanked it toward the floor. With a cry, Geneva released it. As it clattered to the floor, Jenna's cousins rushed toward the back door. They threw it open and ran out.

Jenna checked the gun and took out the bullets. Putting them on the table, she saw Abe's grin as a voice called from the backyard, "You're under arrest."

The scene at the Rickaboughs' farm wouldn't be normal for hours, Abe knew. The police had taken one look in the nearest chicken house and called the Society for the Prevention of Cruelty to Animals. Between the vans that had come to take the dogs and puppies to where they could be evaluated and treated and the cruisers flashing their lights like a blue-and-red lightning storm, he guessed the police would be there most of the night. Some local cops were out on the road, directing traffic and keeping the curious away.

"So far they've found over three hundred dogs alive." Abe crossed the wet grass. The thunderstorm had missed them, but the rain hadn't.

"I had no idea that many were in the barns." Jenna stepped aside to let a volunteer carry two more puppies to a waiting van.

He was glad the twins were sitting on the front porch with Buddy and Pal where they wouldn't witness what was happening in the back. The twins were busy talking to the dogs about the playtime reward Buddy had earned. They'd been as enthralled as the dog at seeing him play.

Abe wished he could set aside his still breath-squelching fear as he thought of how the twins' innocent walk with Pal had led them to the Rickaboughs' farm. Seeing the open door on the barn, they'd gone inside to see what they could discover. Geneva had found them there and forced them into the house, realizing she had in them the perfect way to make Jenna sign over her *grossmammi*'s farm. She must not have noticed Pal who remained behind among the cages.

"The cops have got one more barn to check," Abe said, trying to focus on the here and now where his littlest brother and sister were safe, "and as soon as they get a search warrant, they're going into the house."

"They won't find any dogs there." Jenna glanced toward the house. "Geneva might have lied about a lot of things, but she didn't lie about hating dogs. Thank you, Abe, for calling the cops. I know you have your reasons for not doing so before, but—"

"Ah," interrupted a deep voice out of the darkness. Abe recognized the police chief's voice. "Just the person I've been looking for. Can I speak to you, Jenna?"

"Of course." She put her hand on Abe's shoulder for a moment before she walked away to talk to the chief. It was long enough for him to savor the warmth of her trembling fingers.

Trembling?

Her hands had been steady while she'd confronted her cousins. Had her courage been built on a foundation of fear like his own? That was an eye-opening thought. He'd seen fury blazing in her eyes. Yet, she held it in. As she'd held in so many things since the explosion that had torn apart more than her and Buddy's legs. It had ripped the very fabric of her identity, but she patched herself together so the pain couldn't seep out past her wounds.

Abe saw Jenna nod, smile and then shake the chief's hand. Art's face creased in a wide grin before he walked to where his officers had put one Rickabough in each patrol car. Jenna returned to the porch with the twins and her dogs in tow.

"Everything okay?" Abe asked.

"Art assures me it will be." She smiled at Abe's sister and brother. "The twins are okay, and the Rickaboughs will have to face justice. It'll take some time for the wheels of justice to turn, but they will."

She held her hands out to Zeke and Zoe. When the twins threw their arms around her waist, she rocked backward into Abe. He put his own arms around her and his youngest siblings. He didn't want to let any of them go, but wasn't sure how he could hold on to them forever.

Chapter Sixteen

The next morning, Abe walked into the kitchen when Jenna called to him. His steps were slow, but he'd catch up on sleep in a few days.

He hoped. So many changes in so little time. He couldn't believe all that had happened since yesterday afternoon. He gave Jenna a weary smile as he closed the screen door. The storm last night hadn't eased the heat or the humidity.

"You look more rested than I feel, Jenna."

"You do look pretty much like roadkill this morning."

"Such a compliment."

"Hey, you know I'm always going to be honest." She didn't give him a chance to respond before she asked, "A cup of coffee?"

He nodded. "Or better yet, the whole pot."

Motioning for him to sit, she filled the coffee maker and started it. "Have you had breakfast?"

"*Ja*, but hours ago."

"I've got some ham and onions. How about an omelet?"

He gave her a cockeyed smile. "Are you cooking?"

"I've gotten better."

"Let me be the judge of that."

After silent grace, Abe ate the omelet as well as toast and some fruit she'd cut. When she arched a brow as he paused to take another drink, butterflies did a synchronized flying act in his middle.

"You're improving, Jenna."

"Or you're starving."

He took another piece of toast and forked some omelet on it. "No, you're improving. You're not the only one. *Daed* and *Mamm* and I spent last night talking. I'm not sure exactly when they realized their mistake in putting their business ahead of their family. It could have been when we caught Benuel and Homer or when my brothers admitted to slashing your tires because they knew you and the dogs wouldn't be home on Fourth of July night."

"Why did they do that?"

"Apparently because they were bored. Trust me. They're going to be so busy for the next few years they won't have time to be bored."

"I'm glad your parents have come to their senses."

"I hope they have. Right now, I was the one who's doling out punishment for Homer and Benuel, but my folks were upset to learn what they'd been doing. Then they discovered how the twins were put in danger by Daryl and Geneva. On top of that, Sara Beth told them about her pregnancy scare."

"So she was honest with them about having ovarian cysts? She did explain they were benign, and that the doctor wants her to return in a few months so it can be determined if the cysts have gone away or changed?"

"*Ja*, she did, as well as saying that the cysts often vanish on their own." He reached for more milk to put in his *kaffi*. "The fact they didn't know their own daughter feared she was pregnant warned they need to try to spend more time with their family. They're talking about hiring additional help. I may have convinced them that talking to their *kinder* during meals is more important than customers."

"They agreed?"

Hearing the disbelief in her voice, he was relieved he wasn't the only one worried his parents' change of heart would be temporary. "*Ja*, but we'll see how it goes. Old habits are hard to break."

"You've broken one of your own already. You've spoken up on behalf of you and your siblings instead of taking care of things for your parents." She reached across the table and put her hand over his. "I know how difficult that must have been for you, Abe."

"It was easy." His smile returned. "So easy I should have done it before."

A knock came at the front door. She excused herself.

Abe heard a murmur of voices at the door but couldn't pick out any words. Jenna returned and set an envelope on the table.

"What is it?" he asked.

"*Grossmammi* Dinah's final letter. It was misdelivered. The family was away, and they came home last night to find it." She groped around the table to reach her chair. Behind her, Buddy raised his head, sensing her disquiet. "It's here at last."

He enfolded her hand in his. "As always, God's timing is perfect. Last night, you could honestly tell your cousins you didn't know what was in it."

"Now it's here." Her eyes sparkled with unshed tears. "We can get the answers we've been waiting for."

"Aren't you going to open it?"

"I want to, but what if it announces everything has been left to Daryl and Geneva?"

"Would you deny your *grossmammi* the chance to give the farm to whomever she wishes?"

"Of course I'll do what she wants." She gave an emoted groan. "To give the farm to them—"

He laughed, slicing through her anxiety. "You don't know if that's what the letter says. Open it, and read it. I'm sure whatever is in there will ease your heart, just as the others have."

"Ease? The others have sent me scrambling to find the answers to the puzzles posed in them. Will this one be any different?"

"I don't know. Open it and find out."

She wagged a finger. "Stop trying to pretend you're less curious than I am."

"I don't know anyone who's more curious than I am, though I don't have a horse in this race still. If the farm goes to your cousins, they won't sell it to me, even though they may need the money to pay for lawyers. If it goes to someone else, I'm sure they'll be happy to settle here themselves."

Her face fell. "Oh, Abe, I didn't think about that."

He didn't want to admit he'd thought about little else since yesterday.

She opened the envelope and pulled out pages that were a conventional white. "There are a bunch of pages this time." She took a deep breath. "Okay, here we go…"

"My dearest Jenna,

"How have you done? Have you solved the clues? I'm sure you haven't, because I know the last letter stumped you. I'm sure you got the parts about family, even though you've been so long on your own. I once had high hopes you'd find a family somewhere, a family that supported you as much as you did them. I love your mamm because she was a *gut* wife to my only *kind* and together they brought you into my life.

"Did you get the answers to friends and faith? If you did, did you get them on your own, or did you ask for help? I hope you found help in the barn. Abraham Bontranger is a *gut* man. For his family and for his church. And for you.

"Because Abe is the answer for you when it comes to family, friends and faith. He's strong with all three, and he can show you how to be happy and be loved.

"Don't look so surprised that I believe you two would be a *wunderbaar* match."

"How does she know I'd look surprised?" Jenna asked.

Not sure if she was speaking to herself or to him, Abe remained silent. That way he didn't have to spill his amazement at how Dinah had gauged her *kins-kind*'s reaction. He was grateful she hadn't mentioned *his* reaction to the letter, which spoke of what was in his heart. Every word Dinah had written months—or years—ago were as accurate as if she stood in the kitchen and saw right into him.

"Jenna, when you and Abe were young I saw how much you belonged together, and I'd hoped you'd realize that, too. I know you have many barriers in your way, so I thought I'd remove one by bringing you home to where you should have always been."

There it was. Dinah's plan to have Jenna return to Sweetwater and keep her there long enough so Jenna would want to stay. Had Dinah created this weird will before or after Jenna's near fatal run-in with the bomb? Either way, the older woman had been hoping to reconnect Jenna with the life Dinah had wished she'd always had.

He realized something else, too. The farm was going to be Jenna's. Just as it should have been. He almost asked what she planned to do with it; then he realized he wasn't sure he wanted to hear her answer.

If she said she was staying, he'd want to follow his heart to be with her, but it wouldn't matter. She was *Englisch*. He recalled how he'd seen her talking with Art Damero last night. Had she been talking to the police chief about a job in Sweetwater? Art might be interested in hiring an experienced officer and her canine partner who'd proved his search skills by finding Pal and the twins.

She'd still be a cop.

Or would she want to sell the farm? She might offer to let him have the first chance to buy the property so she could leave. She'd still be a cop.

His dreary thoughts were interrupted when Jenna continued,

"So, my dearest Jenna, don't read any further unless Abe is with you. Share what's in this letter with him. I hope it will answer your questions. How much has he assisted you with following my previous five requests? I don't have to ask, because I've seen for myself how he's been around to help you since you were young *kinder*. Your lives seem to have been meant to go in different directions, though I have never doubted that you two, if you wished, could find a way to walk the rest of your days together. All I've wanted for you, my *liebling*, is joy and the love God has placed right in your path. Maybe this time, you can grasp it, knowing our Heavenly Father longs for you to be happy…just as I do. Whatever you choose, I wish you every happiness. Consider this my last hug."

Tears washed down Jenna's cheeks as she folded the letter and set it on the table. She took the next page off the pile. It wasn't a single sheet. Instead of being handwritten, it was typed.

"It's the deed for the farm." She put the multipage document on the table and smoothed it out. "She's written on it that she left further instructions in her sewing box."

"It's in the living room." He got to his feet, holding out his hand to her. When she took it, he led her out of the kitchen with the dogs following. He pointed to a white-and-blue box on a shelf next to the fireplace. "That's it."

"I know. I saw her using it every summer." Jenna placed the box on the sofa. Unlatching the box, she lifted off the top tray where spools and needles and pins were sorted into the sections. A page popped up like a jack-in-the-box. "It's a Bible verse. No, more than one. From the ninth chapter of 2 Corinthians. Verses six and seven. 'But this I say, he which soweth sparingly shall reap also sparingly; and he which soweth bountifully shall reap also bountifully. Every man according as he purposeth in his heart, so let him give; not grudgingly, or of necessity: for God loveth a cheerful giver.' Under that, she added, 'Share and share alike, Jenna and Abe.'"

"There are more pages in the bottom." He pulled them out and handed them to Jenna.

She flipped them open. Her voice broke. "It's an updated deed with your name on it, Abe. And mine."

"She's left the farm to both of us?"

Abe's shock was so genuine and sweet Jenna had to fight more tears.

"That's what she meant by share and share alike." She handed him the papers.

He gave them back when he'd finished scanning the pages. "I can't believe it."

"Why not? *Grossmammi* Dinah had the biggest heart of anyone I ever met. She made mittens for my sister who never appreciated them. She welcomed me here when my mother's career moves meant I'd lost my home again. She gave you a haven when your family overwhelmed you. You must have told her about your dream of having a farm."

"*Ja.* A few times." He chuckled. "Okay, a few dozen times."

She tossed the deed onto the sofa before throwing her arms around him. His own enveloped her, and she leaned against him, delighting in the rapid-fire beat of his heart.

Buddy jumped to his feet, and Abe grew still as her partner came toward them. The dog leaned against them, willing to trust Abe with Jenna.

Resting his forehead against hers, he whispered, "Does this mean I've got Buddy's seal of approval?"

"For the moment."

He laughed, his breath caressing her cheek seconds before his fingers did. "Buddy is your K-9 partner, Jenna, and now you're my farm partner."

"The farm has to go through probate, and I'm not sure how long that takes."

"Ken could tell you."

"Or he could tell you. You're just as much an owner of the farm as I am."

"I'm trying to get my head around that fact."

"While you're doing that, let me ask you something else."

"Sure. What?"

"*Ich liebe dich.* I love you. Do you remember the night when I first told you that?"

"*Ja.*" He closed his eyes as he took a deep breath. "I remember what you said, and I remember what I did."

"You laughed." There was no accusation in her voice.

"Not because it was funny. It was because, I've come to see, that I was afraid. I thought laughing would hide my fear from you."

She reached up to curve her hand along his face. "What were you afraid of?"

"Of you." He shook his head. "No, that's not the truth. That's just what I've been telling myself for the past fifteen years. I was afraid of me and how I felt when you said that." He put his wide palm over her hand, holding it to his cheek. "I felt so unworthy because you were the most *wunderbaar* person I'd ever met. When I was with you, everything was right. When you were gone, everything was wrong."

"Do you still feel that way?"

"*Ja.*" The word came out wrapped in longing.

"Then marry me, Abe."

He opened his mouth to answer, then snapped it closed, but his eyes remained wide. "An Amish woman doesn't ask a man to be her husband. She lets the man do the honors."

"I'm not an Amish woman. I was blessed with an Amish grandmother—" she chuckled "—an Amish *grossmammi*, but I'm *Englisch*."

Sorrow washed away his smile. "Which means you must know the answer I have to give you. I was raised plain, and that is the life I've committed myself to."

"Though you haven't been baptized."

"No, but that changes nothing. I can't imagine a life with a TV and a car."

"I'm not talking about things. I'm talking about you and me walking the path *Grossmammi* Dinah believes God wants for us. Something that's partly your way and partly my way. How did she put it? Oh, yeah. Share and share alike." She put her finger over his lips to silence him, then realized there was a better way. Her kiss was supposed to be quick and in jest, but it thrilled her.

With a moan, he pushed her back. "We shouldn't... We can't..."

"Yes, we can." She grasped his hands. "I've got two words for you. Beachy Amish. They're plain, but they drive cars and have electricity in their houses. Most important, they use English at their services."

"They don't have police officers. They're also a peace church, disavowing violence."

"I know. Sara Beth explained about the Beachy Amish the day I took her to the doctor. She tried to give me a quick overview of the various plain sects around Sweetwater, but I understood about a quarter of it. One thing was clear, though. Among Beachy Amish is a place where you'd feel comfortable and that wouldn't be such a huge transition for me."

Sorrow wove through his voice as his eyes burned with

deep emotions. "Jenna, I've no doubt that you can do anything you put your mind to, but you're ignoring the central issue. You're a cop."

"Not any longer. Yesterday when you came looking for the twins, I was putting a letter in the mailbox. That was my resignation from the Philadelphia police department."

"You quit?"

She sat on the sofa. "I did. It's hard to let go of what I believed was the life I was supposed to have. However, God—with some help from *Grossmammi* Dinah—has shown me I've got friends here in Sweetwater, and I love living on the farm…and I love you."

His mouth worked as he struggled to talk. "Jenna, last night you and Chief Damero shook hands. Were you accepting a job with him?"

"He wants Buddy and me to create an area-wide search-and-rescue team. I've checked into it, and there are plain members of search-and-rescue teams in Pennsylvania. You could join if you'd like to work with us."

"After seeing Buddy track the twins and Pal, I don't think I'd want to miss a minute of the fun."

"It's not always fun. You could be tramping through a bug-infested marsh or trying to find your way through a destroyed building or—"

He put a finger to her lips. "Are you trying to talk me into joining you or trying to talk me out of it? You can try to do both, but you can't talk me out of loving you, Jenna."

Joy blossomed as she came to her feet and put her arms around him. "Then let me ask you again. Will you marry me?"

"Whenever you wish." This time, their kiss was not quick or a jest.

Epilogue

The following Tuesday, there was no letter from *Grossmammi* Dinah. It was painful, because Jenna knew her grandmother had contacted her for the final time. At breakfast, before Abe went to the barn—*their* barn—to do chores, the two of them had prayed together. She loved the way he spoke with God, and she was trying to do the same herself. It was simpler, she'd discovered, than trying to restrain her wild curls beneath a *kapp*. The minister they'd talked with on Sunday had suggested she wear the white cotton veil that draped over the back of her head rather than the circular mesh *kapp*.

Jenna was pinning it into place for the fourth time that day, because it kept falling off her curls, when she heard gravel crunching and whirled. A Mercedes she didn't recognize came along the drive. She couldn't think of anyone in Sweetwater who drove such a fancy car. Most people had trucks like she did or SUVs or buggies. Could it be her sister arriving? Despite Susan's promise, no text with an itinerary for the Gasteyer family had ever popped up on her phone.

The car slowed to a stop behind her truck, and the doors opened. Four people and two French bulldogs emerged from the car just as Abe came out of the barn, curious about who'd arrived at the farm.

She wanted to let her eyes rivet on him while he walked

toward the house so she could admire his graceful stride. In-stead, she looked at the car.

"Susan!" she cried as the woman with two young kids took a single step toward her. The man, whom she recognized as her brother-in-law, Dustin Gasteyer, stayed by the car as if he wasn't sure if he'd be welcomed on the farm.

Or to make a quick getaway, because it was clear none of the people in the yard wanted to be there. The adults stared at the ground, and the children clung to her sister, peering around her.

Jenna hurried to them, smiling at her nephew and niece. Harper was the perfect age to play with Zeke and Zoe, and she was sure she could find playmates for Liam.

Then she raised her eyes to look at her sister, and she couldn't silence her gasp. She couldn't remember ever seeing Susan with her makeup messed and every hair not perfect. Her sister's eyes were ringed with pink, a sign she'd been weeping, and lines were drawn in her smooth forehead.

Jenna threw her arms around her sister. "I'm so glad you're here."

"We had no place else to go."

"There are always choices." She glanced at Abe, who had stopped a few feet away. "I'm glad you made the decision to reach out to me."

"Like I said, I had no other choice. The people I thought were my friends turned their backs on us. It was as if they'd never known us to begin with."

"Then they weren't true friends. Your friends are with you through thick and thin. Just as your family is."

Tears flooded Susan's face, and for the first time in too long, Jenna saw the little sister who'd once been her dear-est friend.

"Thank you, Jenna. You don't have any reason to take us in after how I've treated you."

"You've treated me like sisters treat one another. We may not always be close at hand, but we're always close at heart."

Susan nodded, unable to speak.

When Jenna held out her hand to him, Abe walked closer. She clasped his hand and brought him into the conversation. "Susan, this is Abe Bontranger."

"The infamous Abe?" Susan flushed. "I'm sorry. I'm all over the place today. Nice to meet you, Abe. Jenna has told me a lot about you."

He chuckled. "It sounds as if she did. She told me a lot about you, too. She missed you when she was here, and she spoke of you often."

"You did?" Susan's voice was a piteous mew.

"I did." Jenna smiled. "Abe and I are getting married sometime next year." She didn't add that they were going to take lessons in preparation for baptism. After that, they could set a date for their wedding. "We already have a family." She put her fingers to her mouth and whistled.

Buddy and Pal ran toward her, Pal almost falling on every step while Buddy's motions were elegant. After introducing them to her sister, her husband, their dogs and to Harper and Liam, who didn't need urging to run off to play with the tire swing, Jenna invited her sister and Dustin into the house. The dogs sniffed each other, then acted as if they'd known each other their whole lives and ran together to join the kids on the tire swing. Abe went to help Dustin with their bags, but they hadn't brought much. Knowing her sister, Jenna suspected there would be a whole lot of boxes delivered to the house in the coming days.

Later, while the Gasteyers were getting comfortable in their rooms, Jenna was squeezing lemons for lemonade to enjoy before supper. Rain battered the windows, and she hoped it would break the humidity. She would have to drive into town tomorrow to buy more fans for the bedrooms.

"Look!" Abe pointed out the window. "A rainbow."

"A double one!" She grabbed his hand and walked out onto the porch where they could admire the huge horizon-to-horizon twin arcs. "God's promise He's here with us always."

Abe put his arms around her and drew her to him. "God's promise that he loves us. Just as I love you, *liebling*."

As he kissed her, shouts came from upstairs along with the sound of feet pounding the stairs. They moved out of the way as Harper and Liam burst out onto the porch, chattering about the rainbow.

Abe looked over their heads and winked at her. They had families who would continue to complicate their lives, but it was a challenge they would face together with laughter and with love.

* * * * *

Dear Reader,

Welcome to the Eastern Shore of Maryland where horses have an island and the rivers run with black water. It's a beautiful place with the Atlantic Ocean on one side and Chesapeake Bay on the other. Though Ocean City is filled with tourists, eager to enjoy the sandy beaches, the rest of the area is dotted with farms growing soybeans and corn for the millions of chickens raised there. Quiet farms and tree-shaded back roads show why the Amish have moved there. Not that Jenna Shetler planned to move there when she came to settle her Amish *grossmammi*'s estate. On the other hand, Abe Bontranger can't imagine living anywhere else. Falling in love complicates their lives in ways they couldn't have imagined... but isn't that what love always does?

Visit me at www.joannbrownbooks.com. And look for my next book coming soon!

Wishing you many blessings,
Jo Ann Brown